Heart of the Castle:
A Ghost Story

Heart of the Castle: A Ghost Story
By R. Fulleman
Editor: Suzie Haughton
Interior Formatting: Marian Oprea
Cover Illustration: Rengin Tumer
Distributed by: LorRonCo
www.LorRonCo.com

Educators and librarians, for a variety of teaching tools
visit us at www.LorRonCo.com

(HOTC Ghost Story: Reading Level=4.0, Flesch Reading
Ease=89.7%, 46K words - Lexile: 710L
HOTC True Story: 2K words)
(Ghost Story Series: Bk. 2)

Summary: 15-year-old Katie travels with her friends to summer school in Romania. There, she must get the help of ghosts to find gold hidden in Transylvania's Bran Castle before a dangerous ex-secret policeman can find it.

Library of Congress Control Number: 2022922013

ISBN: 978-0-9886434-3-7

Printed in the United States of America

Heart of the Castle: A Ghost Story

R. Fulleman

LorRonCo

Other Books by R. Fulleman

Ghost Stories:

Ron and Bob Stories:

Table of Contents

Table of Contents

Table of Contents

Acknowledgements

Thanks to my daughter, Suzie, whose inspiration in wanting to know her own Romanian roots and whose patience and suggestions allowed me to complete this story. To my Romanian mother, grandmother, and ancestors. Te iubesc din toată inima. Thanks to my lovely wife who had to listen to too many "what do you think of this change I made" questions, and my son, Greg, who helped so much with the amazing cover. Additionally, thanks to fellow writer, Joanna Pendleton, for her encouragement and suggestions, along with my daughter-in-law, Grace. Lastly, thanks to Castul Bran, who allowed me to use their floor plans.

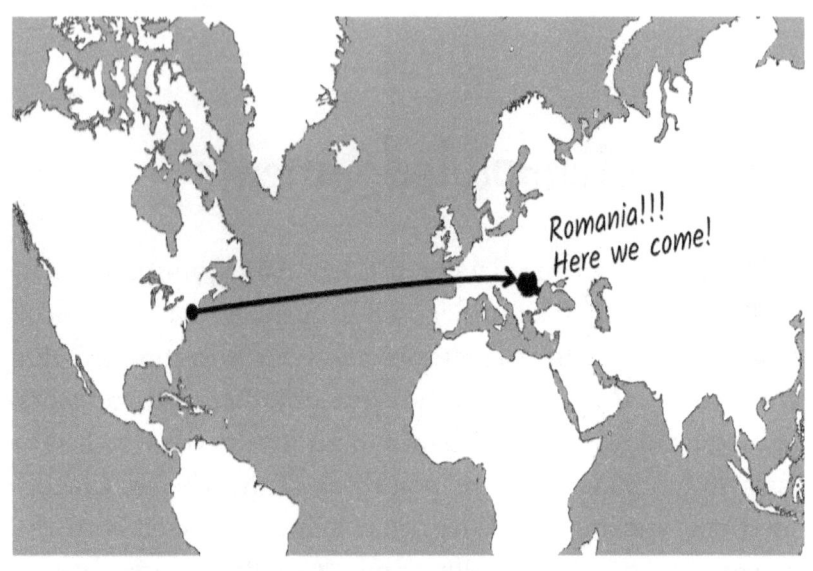

Romania!!! Here we come!

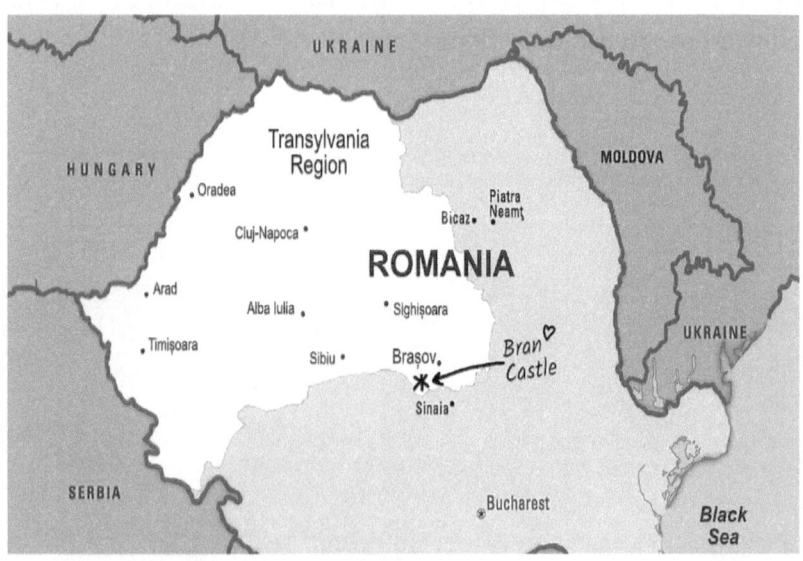

SUMMER PLANS

Chapter 1

"Tell me you're going to Transylvania with me this summer," Katie announced before she got all the way into the coffee shop. She was so excited to tell her two best friends, Cam and John, about her plans that she couldn't wait any longer. Cam and John quickly looked up from their drinks. Everyone in the shop stopped talking and looked up, too. In Katie's excitement, she said it louder and quicker than she had intended. But, if Katie had noticed some of the odd looks given her, she didn't show it. Katie was a very confident 15-year-old girl and she was on a mission to let her friends know about this new adventure she planned.

The boys had their drinks and had just sat down at their usual table. They had gotten to the coffee shop on time to hang out with Katie. They were surprised that, for once, Katie was right on time, too. Normally, Katie was a few minutes late. She liked to be "fashionably late." Katie thought it made her a little more interesting. Also, she didn't want to be too predictable. The funny thing was, she was predictably late most of the time. In spite of that, she was a good person to have as a friend, always there for whoever needed her. It was one of her quirks.

"Transylvania? Isn't that where all the vampires are?" John asked. "Are you into vampires now?"

Dressed, as usual, in all black with a large white skull on his t-shirt, John looked like the one who would go looking for vampires. He was tall for his age and thin. His black clothes made him seem even thinner than he was.

"Of course not! There are no such things as vampires. We all know that. That's made up stuff," she said. Katie believes in ghosts, but vampires? No way!

"You've got to admit, it would be more of an adventure than staying around here all summer. And, if we happen to find some ghosts, that would be great too," she said with a sly look on her face.

John's eyebrows went up when Katie said 'ghosts'. Katie could tell that got his attention. Katie and John have been close friends since they met in 8th grade because they both have an interest in ghosts. Then, last year, Katie met John's friend, Cam. He had a ghost problem that they were able to help him with.

Fifteen-year-old Cam swept his hand through his light brown hair. He stayed quiet for a minute. He liked to think things through before speaking. "I know you're into ghosts," he said. "You helped me with mine!" Cam had recently been haunted by the ghost of his grandpa's shipmate from World War II. Cam had been SCUBA diving on his grandpa's sunken ship when he found a ghost that scared him half to death.

Luckily for Cam, all that ended well, plus he and Katie started spending more time together. They barely knew each other before Cam's ghost but are better friends now. Cam didn't mind Katie using the word, 'we'. He wanted to get even closer to Katie but wasn't sure if she felt the same way about him. Also, he didn't want to ruin his friendship with John. Cam knew John wasn't seeing anyone. He just didn't know if John also wanted Katie to be his girlfriend. He could never build up the courage to ask John about it.

Katie bought her drink and sat down with the boys. They hunched over the small table while Katie spoke. Katie's next words brought Cam back into the conversation. "There's more. I'm going to go to summer school there. I am hoping you guys will be going too, right?" she asked. Katie looked at her two silent friends and focused on their eyes; first she looked into Cam's good natured blue eyes. Then she looked into John's questioning brown eyes. Katie always says the eyes are the windows to the souls.

John looked at Katie again with raised eyebrows. His eyebrows said a lot more than what was coming out of his mouth. They said, *Wow, that might be cool.* But, out loud he said, "I, I don't know what my parents might say."

"Come on, John. This will be perfect for us. There's even a field trip to a castle nearby. They say it's one of the most haunted castles in the world. They've had all kinds of sightings there. It was built in the 1300s so there's bound to be some ghosts floating around there," Katie told John.

Cam knew Katie mentioned ghosts again to give John more reason to come on the trip, but that wasn't the case for Cam. Cam did want to spend time with Katie and he didn't want to be left out . . . *but ghosts, did it have to be ghosts?* He was beginning to understand that to hang out with Katie, ghosts would be involved somewhere.

Cam couldn't give Katie an answer, not yet anyway. "I don't know if I can, but at least I already have my passport. My parents are going to want to know everything about this trip before they say yes. Tell us more," he said. "How much will it cost? When are you going? When will I need to tell you if I can go?"

John's mind was slowly coming up to speed. "Wait, passport? Isn't Transylvania in the United States?" he slowly asked. He tried to remember his 7th grade World History lessons.

"Are you thinking of Pennsylvania?" Katie asked.

"Oh, yeah," John replied, bumping his head with the palm of his hand. "I didn't remember hearing about any haunted castles in Pennsylvania."

"Ok. Let's start with the basics. Romania is in Europe. Transylvania is an area in the country of Romania. It used to be a part of Hungary, but that was a long time ago," Katie said in a way that sounded as if everyone should know that. "My relatives were farmers or something like that. They lived in Transylvania. They didn't have a lot of money or anything. So, before World War II, my great-great-grandma came here, to the U.S. The bad thing is she died not long after getting here. Her daughter was young, so she didn't know much about her family. I've learned all I can about them from my grandma who researched them. I still want to learn more about that side of my family."

Cam felt as though he had slept through his history and geography classes. He didn't remember hearing Transylvania mentioned at all. He felt sure he would have remembered if he had heard of it in school. He only heard of it in old vampire movies. He also felt bad since he should have known his friend better.

"Oh, that's right. Your family is from there. I forgot you are part Romanian." he told Katie.

With her head slightly tilted and her slow nod, she said a lot. Her nod said, *Cam, you should have known this.* And at the same time, it also said, *how could you not think Transylvania was a real place?* "I don't know about you," she said as she shook her head. "I may have to insist you come with me so you'll learn something," she teased.

Katie reached across the table, taking hold of Cam's and John's hands. She gave them each a short squeeze. She wanted her two friends to go with her on the trip. She knew it would be more fun for her if the boys went, too. If they went, it would also help her get permission to go. Her dad wasn't so open about her going alone. Katie knew her mom and dad liked Cam and John. Her parents were the ones who encouraged Katie to ask Cam and John to go with her. They felt Katie would be safer in a group of close friends rather than being there with only strangers.

Katie glanced at Cam. She wasn't looking for this trip to bring her a big romance. Of course, if Cam was there, she would prefer a romance with him rather than one with a Romanian stranger.

"Students stay in the college dorms. They're like little apartments for one or two students. I'll bet it will be cool even just to stay in the college dorms." Katie had high hopes of what the rooms looked like. She always imagined them being cool like in the movies. "The classes are given at the college."

Cam and John both wondered how much studying they would need to do. They generally thought summer should never involve school. John thought even regular school should barely involve studying.

Katie could read their faces. "You won't really have to put much effort into the classes. I read that the classes are for only a few hours each day. The rest of the day everybody goes on field trips or gets to explore the town. There's no pressure. I thought it sounded like a lot of fun. All the meals are included. You're basically taken care of."

Most of it sounded good to both the boys. The part about going to school during their summer vacation was the only bad part for them. John and Cam had to talk their parents into letting them go with Katie. Finally, both got permission to go on their summer adventure.

I LEARNED IT ALL FROM TV
Chapter 2

C am's mom and dad wanted to learn more about where Cam would be going. They did not know much about Romania. One night, Cam found his mom and dad watching a PBS show on TV. It was all about lost Romanian gold.

"This is interesting, honey," Cam's mom told him as he walked by the couch. "You should watch this since you're going there this summer."

Cam got a bowl of ice cream and sat down on the couch next to his mom to watch the show too. It said that thousands of years ago the people who lived in Romania, called Dacians, had lots of gold that the Romans came to take away. The people hid the gold, and the Romans didn't find most of it. It's been lost ever since. People are still looking for it. That night, Cam texted Katie and John and told them the story of the lost gold.

JOHN: OMG thats crazy! what if we found the gold

JOHN: its probably in some old castle. We'd better check out ALL the old castles

JOHN: thatd be so cool! It would be total payback for having 2 go 2 school during summer

JOHN: ghosts treasure awesome!

KATIE: their government doesnt let anyone keep things like that

KATIE: we'd probably end up giving it all to them. bsides think of how many people have already looked 4 it

KATIE: no way we be the ones to find it

John lost some of his energy.

JOHN: who knows?

JOHN: if we find it maybe a few coins might end up @ the bottom of my suitcase

JOHN: that wouldn't be so bad

Cam didn't think they had a chance of finding any 'lost gold'. *Still, it would be nice to dream about it*, Cam thought.

CAM: maybe they'd let us pay 4 the trip at least

KATIE: maybe

There's no way we'll find that gold, Katie thought.

KATIE'S GOING AWAY GIFT
Chapter 3

The big day finally came. Katie was late, again. This time it was mostly her mom's fault. Before leaving the house, she called Katie to her room. Katie's grandma was already sitting in the room.

"Just think, Katie," her grandmother told her. "You're taking the biggest trip of anyone in the family other than *Bunică* Anna. You remember me telling you about her, don't you? *Bunică* means grandmother in Romanian. She's my grandma and your great-great-grandma. She came all the way to America with her little girl. That was a long trip, especially back in the 1930s.

"Didn't her husband come too?" Katie asked.

"No, her husband died before she left Romania. I think that's part of the reason she came here. She was lucky that her brother had come to America a few years earlier to live. I'm sure I told you how she died not long after getting here. Poor thing, being hit and killed by a car when she was crossing a street. She came to start a new life, and it ended before it started.

At least her brother, Cornel, was a good man, taking her daughter, Victoria, and raising her as his own," her grandma said. "He was as close to a loving grandpa that I could have asked for."

"It must have been hard for a single woman with a young child to travel so far. She probably had really good reasons to make that change in her life," Katie's mom said. "I mean, to leave friends and family, almost everything, to come to America."

"She sounds brave. I'm sorry you never got to know her, Grandma," Katie said.

"I agree," Katie's mom said. She then gripped the jewelry box sitting on her lap and gave it a gentle shake. Katie had seen the box when she came into the room, but now wondered why her mother had it on her lap. "Katie, your grandma and I have a present for you."

Katie's eyes showed her surprise. "What is it?"

"We can't go with you, but we wanted you to have a piece of the family with you. Your grandma and I want you to take *Bunică* Anna's necklace with you on your trip. We thought it would be a fitting tribute for you to wear something that means so much to us, and to *Bunică* Anna."

"This was one of the only things *Bunică* Anna brought with her, besides her daughter, Victoria, of course," Katie's grandma said.

Katie's mom lifted the necklace out of the jewelry box and held it up.

"I remember seeing this before," Katie said. "You've always said it's lucky, didn't you?"

"Yes," Katie's mom said. "It has been for me."

"What's that shape exactly? It looks sort of like a wolf's head, but not like one I've ever seen," Katie asked.

I'm pretty sure it's something special to Romania," Katie's Grandma said.

"Wow, great-great-grandma Anna wore this necklace," Katie said. "I never knew it was hers."

"Yes, and now it will be returning to Romania with you," her grandma said. "We hope it will be lucky for you and keep you extra safe."

"But, are you sure? I'm kind of worried about wearing it. What if something happens to it?" Katie asked, carefully holding the necklace in her hand.

"I know you'll take good care of it," Katie's mom said.

"Okay, but I'm still going to be nervous wearing *Bunică* Anna's necklace on the trip. Hey, I'm just nervous about going to Romania and trying to fit in. I identify most with the Romanian side of our family, but it's been so long since anyone actually lived there. Will anyone in Romania even consider me as being the least bit Romanian," Katie said.

"Our family is from Romania, so you are Romanian enough," Katie's grandma reminded her.

"At least your grandma has taught you a few words of Romanian. That should help," Katie's mom added, trying to make her daughter feel a little better.

Katie wasn't so sure that knowing a few words in the language would make anyone think she's Romanian.

"I wish I knew more about Romania and our family there. The little I do know about, happened such a long time ago."

Just then, they heard, "Olga, come on! We're going to be late, as usual," as Katie's dad called up to his wife.

"We'll be right down," Olga called back down.

"I have a favor to ask of you, Katie," her grandma said, "If you get to the city where *Bunică* Anna lived, please visit her grave, if you can. After she died, her brother decided it would be best to send her body back to be buried in her homeland. The cemetery is somewhere in the city of Bran. Please give her my love."

"We will have some free time to do whatever we want, so I'll do my best to find it." Katie said.

Her mom added, "Even if you can't find the grave you'll probably get to walk along some of the exact streets your family did 100 years ago. That's something, right?"

"It is," Katie said.

As the women all stood up, Katie slipped the necklace on and gave the golden medal a tight squeeze, right before she gave her mom a big hug.

"Thanks, Mom. I'll take good care of it," Katie said. "I can't wait to start this trip!"

"Olga!" Katie's father shouted again.

"We're just coming down now," Katie's mom shouted as she started down the hall.

"Say "hi" to my grandma for me," Katie's grandmother said quietly, just to Katie. "You know, grandmothers and granddaughters have a pretty special bond." She gave Katie an extra squeeze before she went back to her own room.

Katie tucked the necklace down in her shirt. She thought it might be safer inside her shirt than on the outside. Then she hurried down the stairs.

Katie and her parents got in their car and headed for the airport.

Cam's and John's families drove to the airport in separate cars. They all met up at the drop-off area.

The parents walked their kids to the ticket counter, got the tickets, and said their goodbyes. The kids were ready to board the plane.

John knew this was going to be the biggest trip of his life. He'd never been so far from home before. Katie had flown to California once when she was a little girl. She knew it wasn't as long as this trip would be and she was so excited, it didn't matter to her how long it would take. Cam was pretty calm. He knew he was in for a long flight.

HOW DO YOU SAY THE NAME OF THIS TOWN?

Chapter 4

Everyone was tired by the time they got to Romania. For Cam, leaving the airport and getting to the train station was a bit of a blur. He was happy Katie took charge.

With the help of a taxi driver who spoke English, they went right to the train station.

They were surprised to find the person selling the train tickets also spoke English. "Maybe we don't need to learn the language after all," John joked.

After some time on the train, John looked at his ticket. "Wait! We're on the wrong train! It says, Brașov. I thought we're going to Transylvania." he said.

"Didn't you read the travel plan I made for you?" Katie scolded playfully. "The school is in the city of Brașov. Brașov is in the area called Transylvania."

"I read it!" Cam quickly said, half raising his hand. "I have to say I'm glad I didn't have to be the one to write out all the travel info we'll need. That had to be a lot of work."

"You're welcome, Cam," Katie said, even though Cam hadn't actually thanked her. She spoke to Cam, but was looking at John.

"Oh, and to make it clear, Brașov is pronounced like Bra-show-v." She realized she was probably going to get annoyed with John many more times throughout the trip. Thinking of past adventures with John, he had always done some things that annoyed her, but he was always there for her whenever she needed him. She'd forgive him as she had in the past. Though, she did wonder what else John hadn't learned about their trip before coming half way around the world.

It was dark outside now. The light in the train compartment made the window reflect like a mirror. Katie was glad to use the "mirror", but not so glad how tired she looked. She used her fingers as a comb to bring some life back into her flattened hair. She had some hair clips and a brush in her bag but didn't want to take the time to find them. "I wish we could have gotten here in the daylight so I could see the countryside," she said. "I've been told it's pretty. This isn't the start of the trip I dreamed of."

WE CAN'T KEEP MEETING LIKE THIS, CAN WE?
Chapter 5

Katie had just stood up when the train gave a short lurch. She was immediately thrown back down to the bench. She fell right into Cam's arms. He had never been quite that close to Katie before. He paused for a moment before letting her go. "We can't keep meeting like this," he said out loud. He blushed a little. He didn't mind Katie falling into his arms. He thought, *Wow, I'm glad I didn't drop her. She'd have thought I was a real wimp.*

Katie turned a bit red and stood up. She jumped over to the opposite bench and sat down. "I think you're right," she said, looking down to hide her face. To change the subject, she gave a quick glance out the window. "Looks like we might be here."

At last, the train came to a complete stop. The bright lights on the train platform were a big change from the dark train car. Outside stood a large sign, BRAŞOV.

The trio stood up and took their bags down from the overhead rack. John and Cam felt a bit lost. They didn't understand any of the languages they heard around them. *I hope you remember your basic Romanian, Katie,* Cam thought.

"Now, to figure out how to get to dorm #10. No," she said, mostly to herself. "I need to start thinking in Romanian. *Căminul* 10," Katie corrected.

"Dorm 10?" John asked. "Don't we need to find the school first?"

"No, their letter said to check in at the dorm first. I mean *Căminul*," Katie said.

Katie spotted a man inside the station holding a sign that read, Summer School / *Cursa de Vară*. Other teens in the station came up to read the sign. The man spoke in English, "Please, students for summer school, we will get on the buses when everyone is here."

Katie felt mixed emotions. *People speaking English does make it easier for me to find what I'm looking for. But, will I ever be able to use the Romanian I'll be learning? This can't be how it was when my family lived here.*

WE'RE JUST DOWN THE HALL
Chapter 6

Fifteen minutes later, the bus came to a stop. All the students got up to leave the bus. Katie, Cam, and John followed down the aisle of the bus to its door.

"Thank you," Katie said to the driver, forgetting to say it in his language. Then, she remembered. Before she could say it in Romanian, the driver gave a nod and a smile in return. Katie smiled, but as she walked away, she shook her head.

Cam saw her and sensed her frustration. "What's wrong?"

"Oh, it's just that I haven't used any of the Romanian I know yet. Almost everyone speaks English. I thought speaking the language would be a big part of me connecting to my family."

"I'm sure we'll find more than enough people who don't speak English here. But, remember, it's not exactly what you say," Cam said. "It's really how you say it. Most people know when you're trying to say 'thanks'."

"Yeah, I guess you're right," Katie said. "I wish I could speak it more, with somebody."

John was still trying to understand all the new things he had seen so far, so he was fine with more people speaking English.

A line formed, stopping inside the doorway of the dorms. There, a woman sat at a small desk with a list of the students. She checked them off as they told her their name and she handed them a key to their rooms.

Cam and John let Katie in front of them in line. They both figured they needed Katie to go first. That way, she could probably help them when it was their turn.

Katie's time at the desk was short. Slowly, and pronouncing every part of the words, she said, "My friends and I came here together. Can we have rooms near each other?"

The woman paused to think what Katie said. The woman spoke some English, but not a lot. Finally, the words came to her, "Yes, only few doors apart."

Again, Katie said, "Thank you" and the lady nodded. *Maybe there's hope for me to use the Romanian I will be learning yet*, Katie joked to herself.

Katie stepped to the side while Cam and John both told the lady their names. The lady gave the boys one key because they were sharing the room. Then, she waved the boys away so she could help the next student.

Katie grabbed John's hand to read the room number off of his key. "423," she said. "I'm in 414. I guess the rooms will be close enough. Hey, I wonder if I'll have a roommate," she said.

The boys were glad they were roommates. Katie worried about who she might have to share the room with. "I guess I'll see soon enough," she said.

The teens followed some of the other students who were already going up the stairs.

"At least we're on the fourth floor and not the top floor," John said. John didn't like the idea of walking up so many stairs. He had seen right away there was no elevator.

"Well," Katie said. "It's really on the fifth floor. In Romania, like most of Europe, they don't count the first floor. The counting starts at the top of the first set of stairs."

John's bag felt heavier to him. "Oh no," Cam said. "I hope this gets easier the longer we're here." Cam didn't know about the difference in what the levels were called either.

"I'm sure we'll get used to it," Katie said, as they got to the last step. "Why don't we put our bags down in our rooms? Whoever is done first can meet at the other's room."

"Cool," Cam said. "I can see our room is just over there," and he pointed a couple of doors away.

"Yes, remember I'm in 414. You guys are in 423, right?" she asked.

Cam and John were already at their room. They gave a thumbs up and opened their door.

The first things the boys saw were large windows directly across from the door. Two beds were there on opposite walls. At the end of each bed was a small table and chair. In one corner of the room was a sink.

"Oh, no toilet," John said. "I hope there's one nearby."

"Yeah. I think I saw a sign down at the end of the hall. We can go check that out before we find Katie," Cam said.

Katie's room looked almost exactly like Cam and John's room. She put her bag on one of the beds to claim it, in case she was still getting a roommate. She wanted the bed nearest the sink.

Before Katie could open her bag, there was a knock on the door. She thought it was going to be Cam and John. When she opened the door, she found a short, thin girl with dark skin and wavy hair. The girl wore a large backpack purse and held a suitcase in her hand.

"I hope you speak English," the new girl said.

"I sure do," Katie replied.

The girl's shoulders slumped as a wave of relief came across her face. "Super. Hello, I'm Ruth," she said with a thick accent. "I didn't know who my roommate would be. I know you and I will be the best of friends," she said. It sounded kind of odd to Katie since they'd just met.

"I'm sure we will," Katie replied, already liking Ruth's British sounding accent.

Katie shut the door after Ruth walked in. Ruth saw that Katie had already left her bag on the bed closest to the sink. "I hope you don't mind if I take this bed," Katie said. I'd like to sleep on this side of the room. It's where my bed is at home."

Ruth said, "Brilliant. After all, you got here first and, as luck would have it, my bed at home is on the other wall."

They spent the next 10 minutes putting their things away. Katie couldn't help but notice Ruth had badminton rackets tied on the outside of her large suitcase. "Oh, you must play a lot of badminton," Katie said.

"No, I've never played before," and that was all she said about it.

OK, Katie thought to herself, *Ruth is going to be one unusual roommate. I can't wait to see what else she's going to pull out of her bag.* Ruth then pulled out a ball of yarn and some knitting needles. It looked as if she was knitting a scarf.

"Do you knit?" she asked Katie.

"No, I never learned," *or had the desire.* The last part she only thought to herself.

"Too bad. My granny gave me this. She started it and only showed me how to do two rows of stitches on it. She said she hoped I'd learn how so I'd have something to keep me busy on this trip."

Katie could only shake her head in disbelief. *Yes, Ruth is going to be some roommate*, she thought. *But, she'll definitely fit right in with my friends.* "We'll have to ask to see if anyone here can give you a hand with that," she added.

Katie went over to room 423. She knocked on the door. No one came to open it. She knew she had taken longer than she intended to get back to the boys, but she had to take that time to talk with Ruth.

After a second or two, Katie heard snoring coming from inside the room. *Those boys fell asleep that fast? I'm glad they made it all the way into their rooms first. We'll talk at breakfast.*

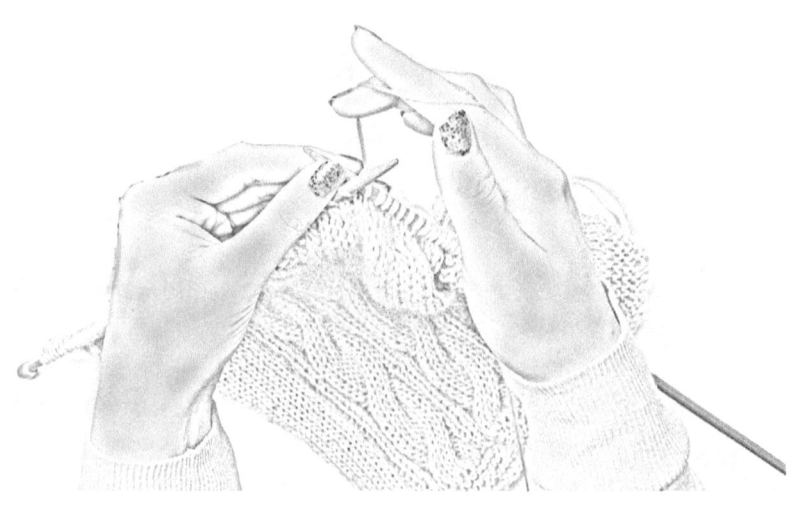

SOMEONE NEW TO THE GROUP
Chapter 7

The next morning, outside their rooms, Katie introduced Ruth to Cam and John. Katie said to the boys, "Oh, please don't let me forget to ask around. I told Ruth that I'd help find someone who knows how to knit. She wants to finish something her grandma gave her to make."

"What are you making, Ruth? I know how to knit," John said.

Katie stood there for a moment with her mouth open and her hands on her hips. Then she said, "What? No way! I can't believe you know how to knit." She was in total disbelief.

"It's cool. Yeah, my grandma taught me years ago. Nothin' real fancy, just simple stitches. Didn't you ever notice the scarves I always wear when it's cold?"

"Of course I've seen them, but I never knew you knitted them. I always thought you bought them, or your mom made them for you."

"I think it's marvelous that you can knit, John," Ruth said looking at him, shyly.

John looked down and said, "It's nothing really. I bet you're better at it than you think."

Now it was Ruth's turn to look down. "I'd love it if you could watch me knit to make sure I'm doing it right."

"Sure, I'd love to watch you! Ah, watch you knit. Give you some pointers," John blurted out before a slight flash of red came to his face.

"Maybe we should go down and find out where we need to go for breakfast first?" Cam said to get their group moving.

Katie got over the surprise of John's hidden skill. "Yes, I'm really hungry. The cafeteria is just next door. Let's go."

The four of them went down the stairs of the dorms and out into the fresh, morning air.

Katie was an unusual girl in her own way. She felt a sense of adventure in most things she did, even just going down to eat. She always thought there was a kind of magic in doing normal things in non-normal places. She could feel it now.

Katie knew that doing common things could be dull. But doing those same things, like eating or going for a walk when you were somewhere new, made it feel different, even special. Katie walked with a spring in her step. She was looking forward to meeting more students. John had gotten over being shy from meeting Ruth. He returned to his old self. He was thinking about what might be on the menu. He was hungry. He was often hungry. At home, he could simply go into the kitchen and grab a quick snack. Here, he didn't have a kitchen to visit. John found himself glancing over at Ruth as they walked. Thoughts of the new girl took over his thoughts of being hungry. He was glad she was Katie's roommate. He knew it would make it easier for him to talk to Ruth. He'd be able to run into Ruth just by hanging out with Katie. He wasn't good at talking to girls.

Once in the cafeteria, John's stomach reminded him how hungry he was. Not knowing anything about Romanian food, he wasn't sure what to expect for breakfast. He had worried that they might serve them some weird food he wouldn't want to eat. John was pleasantly surprised when the food came. There was more food than even he normally ate at home. Though, John didn't expect to see two large tomatoes on his plate, along with sausages, cheese, and bread. Ruth gladly gave John her tomatoes. Her family did sometimes have tomatoes at breakfast in England, but she didn't eat them. For her, breakfast was a little early for tomatoes. John obviously loved them. He ate all of his and Ruth's tomatoes, too. Cam was fine with the food they gave him. He was always flexible about what he ate. That first meal let the students know they would not go hungry this summer.

FIRST DAY AT SCHOOL
Chapter 8

After breakfast, they all boarded an old bus to get to school. It was a short ride from the dorms, just a mile away. All the buildings on the route to the school looked like they were hundreds of years old. The three friends felt like they were in an old movie. As they were riding, Cam made a mental note that there were about 75 students. At the school, the students found their names on lists by each class. Cam, John, and Ruth were in the same class, along with 10 other students. Katie was in a slightly more advanced class.

The other students were friendly. They all said 'hello' or nodded with a smile to Cam and John. The two boys hoped Katie would find friendly kids in her class too.

"Hello class," their teacher said. "My name is Mrs. Popescu. Don't worry. I will start slowly. I know this is your first class in Romanian. I mostly teach history here at this college. This summer, I am teaching you Romanian."

The teacher started out by saying some basic words and getting the class to repeat them. As she was teaching, a man walked in the class and interrupted her. He didn't wait for her to finish what she was saying to the class. He started talking to her in

Romanian. He was around 45 years old with slicked-back black hair. He wore an oddly shiny blue suit and tie. It looked like he wore that suit to be seen as important. His eyes darted over the students as he spoke to Mrs. Popescu. Every time she started to talk, he interrupted her. He never smiled the whole time he was in the classroom. Cam and John wished they could understand what he was saying. All they could make out was their teacher calling him, *Domnul* Lupu.

Without talking to each other, they made up their minds that they didn't care for him. For whatever reason, the man looked like he felt he was the most important person in the room. He didn't act like he cared at all about the students or what the teacher had to say. The adults at Cam and John's school back home were friendly and welcoming. Often, adults there would work to build a good bond with the students.

After class, Katie met up with Cam, John, and Ruth. They all got back onto a waiting bus to return to the dorms. On the ride back, the man in the suit stood up. Putting his hand on a young man sitting up front, he said, "Students. This is Radu. He will be your contact to help you with any problems you have. Go to him first if you have any questions." Then, he sat down without saying anything else. Radu got up, waved to the group, and said mostly the same thing. He sat down and was quiet the rest of the bus ride back to the dorms.

At the dorms, everyone but Lupu went up the steps and into the hall for lunch.

At the table, John was the first to ask, "Who was that guy in the suit? He seemed to be in charge, but not friendly at all!"

Katie added, "Yeah, he came into my class, too. Kind of *slimy* if you ask me. I hope we don't have to deal with him much while we're here."

"I think his name is Lupu. Our teacher called him *Domnul* Lupu. I saw *Domnul* means Mr. in Romanian," Ruth said.

A tall boy at the next table leaned back in his chair. He had heard what was said. Speaking to Katie, he said, "Hello. I'm Deeter. We're in the same class here. I heard you talking about that guy, Lupu. Lupu is the security officer for the school. In Berlin, where I'm from, we saw lots of guys like him. He acts like the old secret police all communist governments had. Maybe you didn't know this, but Romania used to have a communist government. The government held all the power and the people had none. Berlin used to be communist, too. We still have guys like that there. They're dangerous. They don't have the power they used to have, but they act like they do. Be careful what you say around them, yeah, be careful of Radu, too. In the old days, they used to have people like Radu around, pretending to help. But they were watching for students they thought would make trouble."

Cam and John both worried a little. They nodded as Deeter spoke. "Thanks, Deeter," Katie said. "We'll keep that in mind. Oh, I'm Katie, and this is Ruth, Cam, and John," she said as she pointed to her friends.

Glances were exchanged among the four at the table. They ate the rest of their lunch quietly.

There was a group walking tour around the town scheduled for after lunch. All the students looked forward to seeing more of the city. Katie hoped the tour would take her mind off of Deeter's warning.

PAYING HER RESPECTS
Chapter 9

The second day of Katie's classes went smoothly for her. Her teacher had everyone tell the others a little about themselves. She was happy to speak to a girl from France who was friendly.

After class ended, Katie went up to the teacher to ask a question. "Mr. Țoca. Do you know how hard it might be to get to Bran? I have a relative who is buried there, and I thought of visiting while I'm here in Romania."

"It is simple. I know the cemetery there. The easiest way for you to get there is by taxi. It doesn't cost much, and it can take you right there. The ride takes only 15 minutes," he told her.

"I saw some taxi stands here in town, so I know where to get a taxi."

"Good. I will write down the name and address of the cemetery for you to show the driver. And, I will write him a note to wait for you, if you won't be too long. I'm sure the driver will want to wait and be able to return to Brașov."

"That would be great. That way I should be able to go there after lunch tomorrow since we will have free time then.

"Perfect. Here is the note. Oh, there is an office at the cemetery where they can tell you exactly where to find the grave. It's a big cemetery. You don't want to get lost in it," he said, and gave a little laugh. Then, in a more serious tone, he added, "This cemetery has more than its share of stories of strange things going on there. So, be careful where you are walking."

Katie told Cam and John about wanting to go to visit the cemetery, but she left out the warning her teacher had given her. She wasn't sure if Cam would want to come, but she hoped he would. She had mentioned it to Ruth, but Ruth had already made other plans.

"Sure," John said. "Sounds like what I wanted to see here anyway. Is Ruth coming?"

"No, she already said she and some of the other English girls had planned on doing something together tomorrow after school."

John looked disappointed, but he understood.

"Yeah, that'd be fine with me to go," Cam said. "So, you want to go after school tomorrow?"

"Let's eat first and then go," John said.

"Great," Katie said. "Thanks guys. I appreciate you both coming with me. It should be cool, my teacher said it was a big old cemetery. We can get directions where to go once we're there."

IT IS A BIG OLD CEMETERY
Chapter 10

The taxi was easier to get than Katie thought it would be. In no time, the three of them were on their way to the cemetery. It was a quiet ride with Katie, Cam, and John all looking at the countryside the entire way there. The road winded through a narrow valley with high hills on both sides of the road and big trees. The houses they saw were all painted in bright colors. It was all so different from their homes in Maryland.

When they got to the cemetery, the taxi drove through the front gate and parked in front of a small building. The driver spoke English and said he would wait for them outside the office.

Katie led the way into the office and spoke to a person behind the main desk. The woman there drew a small map on some paper and handed it to Katie. Cam was disappointed that the cemetery didn't have a printed map like he'd seen once back home. "This is the old country," Katie joked.

"I hope that lady is a good artist," Cam joked in return. "I wouldn't want to get lost here."

"We'll be fine," Katie said, shaking her head at Cam's bad joke.

They started walking down the paved road that went down the middle of the cemetery with graves on both sides. All the graves they could see had huge headstones. With the many headstones and trees, it was difficult to see far beyond the main road. Plants had grown over some of the graves. It looked like no one was taking care of those graves.

Maybe those graves just don't have any family left to take care of them. I wonder how overgrown Bunică Anna's will be, if we can even find it, Katie thought.

As they walked, they made sure to follow the map the woman drew for them. They were surprised when the road changed from pavement to gravel. The gravel road area appeared darker than the paved road. It took a while for them to notice that it was darker there. Then they also noticed the larger number of trees around them. It made sense to them that more trees blocked out more of the sunlight.

"It looks like this area isn't kept up very well. Are you sure we're going to be able to find the grave?" Cam said.

"And whose grave is this again?" John asked.

"It's my great-great-grandma's, Anna Cristea. She lived around here until she moved to America. She died there, but her brother thought she should be buried in her homeland," Katie said.

The three of them looked over the map again and before long were at the spot that was on the map.

"Oh, my gosh," Katie said. "Look, there it is."

All three walked up to a large piece of stone over a grave. Cut out of the stone was the name Anna Cristea.

"And there's her husband's name, Ion Cristea, right next to hers. I'm glad they're together like this." Katie bent down and pulled up some weeds that were growing over the stones. Cam and John helped by snapping off branches from a bush that was partly covering the headstones.

When they finished cleaning up the graves, Katie knelt down and said a few prayers. Cam and John stood there quietly looking down at the stone. They weren't sure what or even if they should say something. They both decided silence might be best right then.

After finishing her prayers, Katie rubbed her hand across the name carved into the stone and said, "I wish you could have met your granddaughter. She sends you her love." As she did that, a sudden cold gust of wind interrupted her thoughts. "I guess we'd better hurry up and get back to the taxi before he thinks we're not coming back and leaves. Besides, it's getting cold."

"Wait, let me get a picture of you by the grave first, for your family," Cam said.

"Thanks, Cam," Katie said, "I'd like that."

Cam took the picture and checked to make sure it came out alright. "Hold on. Let me take another one. The sun must have hit the lens funny. There's some kind of glare in the picture. I'll take another one."

He checked the camera on her phone after taking the second picture, looked at it, and gave his okay. "Yeah, this one is fine. I don't know what happened with the other one." He then noticed how Katie looked cold in the picture. She was holding her arms as if she was trying to keep warm.

"Are you okay?" asked Cam. "It's not that cold out. It's not really even cool."

Katie made a face at Cam. She thought it was another bad joke from him.

Cam hadn't seen Katie make a face at him. He didn't say anything. Perhaps Katie was just tired. He knew how much it meant to her to find this grave. "Yeah, we'd better get back," Cam said.

As they walked, John said, "Did you see how some of those graves had trees growing out of them? Creepy."

Katie still felt cold all the way to the taxi. Even her necklace felt like ice. *I think it's colder than you tough guys want to admit*, she thought to herself. As the taxi drove back to Brașov through the city of Bran, Katie caught a glimpse of the castle. "Hey, that's where we'll be going this weekend. I can't wait to see it up close."

It was only after they left the city of Bran that Katie warmed up. She wondered if the taxi's heater was on in the summer.

BRAN'S PAST

Chapter 11

Saturday morning brought new excitement to the students. It was their first field trip. The students were being taken to Bran Castle. A visit to Bran was one of the things Katie was looking forward to the most out of the whole trip. She knew her relatives once lived near the castle. Her mom talked about it with her.

"*Buna!*" the teacher said to the students on the bus. "We are on our way to Bran Castle. It has a long history:

The Romanians were not the first people living in this area. They were Dacians. Then, the Romans heard about the Dacians with their advanced society and great wealth. The Dacians were known for their gold. Rome wanted to expand their empire so they decided to take over the Dacians. Roman armies came and fought them to take their gold, but the Romans were unable to find much. That was around the year 100. Later, German Knights were rumored to have found some of the Dacian gold. They were the ones who built Bran Castle as a fortress.

Now, many of you know it today as Dracula's Castle, from the famous book and movies about a vampire named Dracula. But long before those made up things, Dracula was the nickname for a Romanian leader, Vlad Țepes. Dracula is a Romanian word for, 'the little devil.' Vlad was a bloodthirsty ruler who killed many, many souls. Many people believe the castle belonged to Vlad. He only stayed in the castle as a prisoner for a few months in 1462.

Almost 200 years of neglect caused the castle to become run down. Queen Marie fell in love with Bran Castle and the nearby area. Queen Marie was the queen of Romania between World War I and II. She ruled with her husband, King Ferdinand. It was Marie who first had the castle repaired.

Here is a strange fact that many of you may find interesting. The queen loved this area so much she asked that her heart be put in a box and kept here after she died. Her body is buried in a church about a 3 hour drive from here."

Sounds of 'eww' came from all over the bus.

"Oh, gross," John said.

"That's just weird," Cam said.

"Actually, for the last 900 years people have buried hearts away from the bodies. Mostly Kings, Queens, or warriors who died in other countries have done this," the teacher told the students. "Don't let this bother you. It has been moved to another castle."

"Now, if you look through the trees over there, you will see the castle up on the hill."

As Katie looked up to see the castle, she couldn't help but notice a change in the weather from when they left Braşov. In Braşov it was clear, but here dark clouds fill the sky. It gave the castle a scary look as if bad things were sure to happen there.

Cam looked up to see the castle sitting on top of a large rock formation. He imagined invaders trying to attack the castle. It looked impossible. The castle walls seemed to rise straight up into the sky.

"Whoa," John said. A slight chill ran up his back. "Sure looks creepy. If there is a Dracula's castle, that would be it."

"To me it looks kinda cool," Katie said. "But I've read they had a lot of nasty things going on inside. People were violent all throughout history. It was crazy." She looked around and added, "But, of course, that was centuries ago. I don't think it was still that way when my relatives lived here. I wonder what this area looked like then."

Ruth added, "I must say, none of the castles back home look quite like this one. This is definitely a fortress."

"Are there lots of castles back in England?" John asked.

"Yes. We have thousands of castles in England. A lot of them are preserved and still people's homes, but there are hundreds that are abandoned and have fallen down over time."

Katie wondered how it would be to live where there are so many castles. She had never even seen one in person before. She was sure this was the first castle the boys ever saw in person, too.

Once out of the bus and walking to the entrance, they came across a bunch of little buildings. All the stands at the base of the castle sold things like T-shirts and coffee mugs in the shape of a vampire's head. Ruth stopped for a moment in one of the shops and looked over an old photo of a woman wearing a crown. It was Queen Marie.

The queen's crown in the photo caught Ruth's attention. Two other English girls from class stopped to look at the souvenirs with Ruth.

Katie asked one of the leaders of the trip if she would have time to shop after visiting the castle. Once Katie heard that she would, she started straight up the path to the castle. John and Cam put all the effort they could into keeping up with Katie. She was a girl on a mission.

JUST LIKE HOME?

Chapter 12

Once they got up the hill, they took the last set of stairs up to the entrance of Bran. The castle was big, but its low doorways surprised Katie. *Wow, the people who made this castle must have been short,* she thought. She wasn't tall, but she had to be careful to duck when going through most of the doors in the castle.

Katie followed the other students through some small rooms until she saw a door leading to the inner courtyard. She stepped out and saw a large well.

White carved stones made up the sides of the well. A heavy black iron bar gracefully arched over the opening with a large iron wheel hanging from it. The wheel was a pulley that a rope once went through to help people pull up the water bucket.

Katie took in a breath and let it out slowly. She let herself relax a little while she took in the sights of the castle courtyard.

"There you are." Cam said to her. He had been trying to keep up with her. He was glad she finally decided to stop for a minute.

"I thought to take a minute and look around. I don't know why, but I feel like I'm home in this castle."

"You were probably bitten by Dracula in a past life," Cam joked.

Katie responded with a slow shake of her head with an, *I can't believe you said that* look on her face. She didn't take the joke as well as Cam thought she might. He often made jokes. Most of the time his jokes were good, but sometimes his jokes fell flat. He knew right away this was one of those times.

"I don't care about stupid made up stories about vampires!" Katie said, with a little more force than she intended to use.

Before Katie could say anything, Cam said he was sorry. He couldn't remember seeing Katie so edgy.

"It's ok," she said. "Just don't bring it up again, or I might fly into your room and bite you while you're sleeping!" she added with a little laugh. Cam pretended to grab his throat.

Now that things were back on track, Cam suggested they look around some more and maybe find John. He had wandered off some time before they went to the well.

To get back at Cam a little, Katie mentioned ghosts again. "I read that people have seen balls of light and fading images of people down the halls. They said there are poltergeists here, too."

Cam hadn't heard of *poltergeists*. "What's a pole-ter-guys? He asked.

"It's poltergeists. It's a German word. In folk tales, they're ghosts who like to play tricks on people. They'll move things and sometimes break things too," Katie responded.

Cam decided to stay a little closer to Katie after hearing that as they looked for John.

Katie and Cam walked through several rooms in the castle. Though the rooms were all painted white, most of them were dimly lit, with many dark shadows. The halls and stairs were also a bit dim. All the wood was a dark oak that made it seem even older than it was.

Together, those things gave the castle a creepy feeling. Katie looked into every shadow. If there were ghosts there, she didn't want to miss them. But, then again, she also didn't want to be surprised by them, either.

Signs in each room told what the rooms were for or who lived in them. The signs were in several languages.

One room they entered was a bedroom. It didn't have a lot of furniture in it. On one side of the room was a heavy wooden-framed bed. It had twisted posts coming up from each of the four corners. A heavy red bedspread neatly covered the bed. At the foot of the bed was an equally heavy, dark wooden table, but it had a glass case on it.

Under the glass sat a copy of Queen Marie's crown. Across the room was a large tiled heater. It looked kind of like a little oven. The tiles were cream-colored with blue flowers painted on them. Throughout the castle there were other heaters like this.

"Wow, what a pretty crown. The sign says it's a fake one, but they don't say where the real one is now," Katie said.

"Were you looking to claim your crown, your majesty?" Cam joked. "So that's a painting of your relative?" He pointed to a painting of a queen wearing the crown.

"I wish." was Katie's response, followed by a quick, "But, no! I can't even imagine my family seeing the queen."

"The crown is nice, but you wouldn't catch me sleeping in here," Cam said. To him, the room made him uncomfortable. Cam felt like someone or something was watching him, even though he and Katie were the only ones in the room. The castle and everything in it looked so old. All the furniture seemed too dark and heavy. "This place looks like it's waiting for a ghost to move in, if it hasn't already."

"Oh, I don't know," Katie said. "It looks kind of cozy. Of course, I'm pretty sure my parents would never let me decorate my room at home like this."

Katie liked the simple furniture, but she wasn't surprised. After all, the sign in the room said it was the bedroom of Queen Marie. She was the queen of Romania from 1914 until she died in 1936.

Katie stood there for a few seconds with her arms folded. "Wow. Think about it. A queen lived in this room." A cold draft of air came out of nowhere. Katie was about to mention how drafty the castle was when Cam said something.

"I guess I thought everything would be gold inside since it is a castle," Cam told Katie.

Katie forgot what she was going to say. She moved on to Cam's comment. "Yeah, it is a bit simple, but it said this furniture has been here for more than 100 years," Katie replied.

"Come on, Cam. Get in a picture with me," Katie said. She waved for Cam to stand by her.

"Sure," Cam replied. He stepped next to Katie as she fixed her hair. Then, she took a selfie.

"Cam, we're going to have to take another one," Katie said. "There is something too reflective behind us. There's a big glare in the picture." Cam looked to the area of the room where the light came from in the photo. He couldn't see anything there that was reflective. In fact, most of it was just dark brown wooden furniture. A short cool draft of air blew past Katie again.

Katie turned her head to look behind them, too. She also didn't see anything that could have made that glare. Besides, she wasn't using the flash on her camera. "That glare should not have been there. John and I have seen those before in pictures. It may be a reflection, but it may be something more. It may be what I told you guys about. You know, what's been sighted around here."

Oh great, thought Cam. "Here we go again."

Katie knew right away what Cam meant. "Don't worry, Cam. Remember, your ghost wasn't harmful. I'm sure we'll be fine. It may not even be from a ghost."

Despite her words to make Cam feel better, he stayed right by her side. She took his hand. "Wait until John sees this," Katie said, giving Cam's hand a quick squeeze. "I'd better take another picture to see if it happens again." With that, Katie held up her phone and took a quick picture. This time she didn't bother to get in the picture and pointed the phone directly at the area where the glare appeared before.

"Huh?" Katie said. "No glare, just the dark furniture. I'll have to take some more and see how they turn out."

"Oh," Cam said, trying to change the subject and put some distance between them and a possible ghost. "Yeah, we still need to find John. We don't want to lose him. You told his parents you'd bring him back home," he joked. He would be happy to get out of that room and find John. He knew he would feel better to be with both of his friends.

"You go on. I'll catch up in a minute," Katie told him. "You know me. I can't let this go." She hated to tell him to leave when he was obviously nervous, but she couldn't miss a chance to know for sure if it was a ghost or not.

Cam would have liked to have Katie come with him, but he didn't want to stay in that room if he didn't have to. And, he knew he wouldn't be able to get Katie to leave if there was a chance of a ghost being there. Cam started down the stairs, but he didn't like leaving Katie by herself.

Still in the room, Katie stood for a few seconds taking some more pictures and thinking about all the people who probably lived in that room, including the queen. *Could the light in the photo be from a ghost*, she thought? She looked around the room but didn't see anything unusual there or in the other photos.

As Katie was thinking about the photos, she became aware that something was happening. She wasn't sure what she felt. When she did, she almost didn't feel it. Her necklace prickled against her skin. The rest of her felt normal. It was the necklace that felt cold. It was a little odd, but her thoughts went back to her photos.

A bit discouraged, she started for the door to catch up with Cam when she thought she heard someone say, "*Stai.*" "*Stai.*" "*Stai.*" The words were echoing, growing quieter with each word. Her eyes darted around the room. The room was empty. *It might have come from some other room*, she thought. Katie turned again toward the door. Again, she heard the voice, "*nu pleca, nu pleca, nu pleca.*" It was definitely a young woman's voice.

Katie knew it was in Romanian, but she didn't understand it. She didn't know enough yet. But, had to ask herself, *why was it echoing every phrase?*

"Katie! Are you coming?" Cam asked.

Katie stiffened up and her hands jerked open. She hadn't expected Cam to still be there so when Cam stuck his head through the doorway and called her name it startled her.

"We've got to go find John," he reminded her. The truth is he didn't want to wander around the castle by himself looking for John.

"Thanks for the scare, Cam," she said sarcastically. "Is anyone outside?" she asked. "I thought I heard someone speaking in Romanian."

"Oh, sorry. No, not right now."

"That's ok, but I could have sworn I heard someone just say something to me."

"No. I was outside the door and I didn't hear or see anyone," he said. "Maybe it's only the sounds of a very old building?" he offered. "Or, maybe the ghost, or maybe a vampire," he joked.

"You might be right," Katie said. "Not about the vampire, but the old building. I keep feeling drafts. Let's go find John." In her heart, Katie knew she had probably made some contact. For someone interested in ghost hunting like her, this was what she was looking for.

ECHOING THE PAST

Chapter 13

The two moved on to find John. Katie walked slower than normal. She kept looking back over her shoulder. She didn't know what it was, or maybe who it was, she heard. If it was a spirit, would it follow them? she pondered. They finally found John. The torture museum he found after entering the castle had distracted him. He hadn't seen anything else yet.

"You're kidding!" Katie said. "You've been in here this whole time? Really? Cam and I have been through most of the castle already and we found some pretty interesting stuff."

"Well, there's some pretty interesting stuff right here. And, most of the time Ruth was here with me," John said. His face blushed a little red with his last statement.

Katie caught on quickly. John had probably seen everything in the museum before Ruth came in. Then, he stayed with her as if he hadn't seen anything, just to spend time with her, Katie thought. She turned to Cam to exchange a knowing glance, but he looked like he didn't have a clue why John stayed in the museum.

Katie understood. If Katie hadn't been as interested in the castle, she might have done the same if she were in John's place and it was Cam who had walked in.

"Well, we've got the castle down pretty well. We could get you through the highlights pretty fast if you want," Cam said.

"And, we made our first contact with the paranormal," Katie said. She showed John the photo on her phone.

"Whoa, you're right!" he said. He looked excited. "Why don't we go back to the room where you took this picture first?" he asked.

Oh great, Cam thought, a little worried about going back to that room.

"Oh great!" Katie said, anxious to get back to that room.

The three set out at a quick pace so John would have time to take in more of the castle later.

By the time they got to Queen Marie's room, Katie had filled John in on all that had happened there. When they stepped into the room, it didn't look as if anything had changed except the room was brighter. The sun must have moved to a position that let in more light through the windows. John and Katie looked around the room while Cam stood by the door. They didn't find anything unusual so Katie and John were a little disappointed. At that point, Katie was getting a little tired. Her excitement to see everything earlier must have used up a lot of her energy. "You guys go on. There are a few more rooms John hasn't seen yet. Maybe take a few photos and see if any 'body' turns up. I'm going to wait here."

"Ok, we'll be back in a few minutes," John told her. Cam led John out the door and up the nearby stairs.

Once again in the room by herself, Katie felt differently. She felt almost as if she were back home in her house waiting for her mom or grandma to come into the room. The Romanian decorations had a familiar feeling to them.

As Katie looked out the window of the bedroom, she noticed her necklace felt cold again. The air turned cold, too. The sound of a young woman's voice caused her to jump. Katie twisted around to see who the woman was, but she couldn't see anyone there.

The bright light from the window now made it more difficult for Katie to see the inside of the room. Her eyes slowly adjusted to the dimmer light. She strained her eyes to see who had spoken to her. In the darkest corner of the room, Katie could make out the form of a young woman stepping from the shadows.

The woman had dark eyes, dark wavy hair, and a pleasant smile. She wore a white shirt with puffy sleeves. The shirt was like the ones Katie had seen in old pictures of Romania. It had a lot of pretty stitching on it. It was a peasant blouse.

Katie thought the woman might be a guide at the castle.

"Hello?" Katie said.

"Salut. Binevenit," the woman said. "Salut. Binevenit. Salut. Binevenit." Her echoing voice confused Katie. Why is her voice echoing?

Katie was happy she understood the woman saying 'welcome'. In Romanian, Katie said, "Thank you."

"Afară, Afară, Afară," echoed the woman's words.

These last words confused Katie. She didn't understand what the woman said. Also, Katie felt the echoing was creepy. Again, she became aware of how cold her necklace felt. Katie wrapped her arms around herself.

The young woman pointed out the window. Katie glanced over to see what the woman was pointing at. At once, she could feel the woman's presence next to her. Katie felt as if she had walked into the freezer section of her market.

She couldn't stop a cold shiver running through her body. She turned to look back at the woman. A gasp of surprise came out of Katie's mouth. The woman was gone, no longer in the room.

The room felt completely still and quiet. Seeing a ghost that was like a living person was creepier than Katie expected. She wished Cam and John were there with her! Right now!

Katie glanced over the room, straining to search the dark corners again, but she didn't see anyone this time. She hurried to the door. As she got to the doorway, Cam and John came in. The three almost crashed into each other.

"Did you see a woman just leave here?" she asked.

"No, why?" John asked.

"There was a lady over there. I thought she might have been a guide, but I couldn't understand everything she said. She didn't speak English. She was nice enough. But, when I turned to look out the window, she moved near me. I could feel she was very close to me.

Everything instantly felt cold. My necklace was like ice when she showed up. She was gone when I turned back. I have no idea how she could have gotten out of here so fast. And, without a sound," she added. "Unless . . ."

A LITTLE TOO WEIRD RIGHT NOW

Chapter 14

"Was it her voice you heard earlier?" Cam asked. "So, the woman you saw just now had the same voice you heard?"

"I'm pretty sure it was the same. I wish I knew what happened to her. She was just standing there. Where could she have gone so fast? And, you guys didn't see her leave? Whoa, I got goosebumps."

"This is weird," Cam said.

"I'd say this is spooky weird," John said.

Katie and Cam turned to John. At the same time, Katie and Cam said, "Yes, it is."

"This castle is getting a little too weird for me right now. Let's get out of here. Anyway, we're supposed to be back on the buses in a few minutes," Cam said, looking at the time on his phone.

Talking mostly to herself Katie said, "Yeah. I guess I was ready for a shadow, a flash of light, or a reflection in a photo, but not a 'yes, I do look like I did when I was alive' ghost," Katie said.

Wanting to get Katie out of the castle, Cam reminded Katie, "Didn't you want to get some souvenirs before we leave?"

"Oh, that's right. I do need to get some things. Let's hurry," Katie said. "Family first."

Cam found it a little surprising how quickly Katie could switch from ghosts to souvenirs, but she started out the door. He and John knew they had to hurry to keep up with her.

Darting between slow moving people, the three of them ran down the stairs and out of the castle. As she ran, Katie's necklace came out from behind her shirt. The pendant caught on a button and hung with its back side facing out. A symbol that Katie never understood was easy to see by anyone who was in front of her now.

They got to the base of the mountain when Lupu caught their attention saying, "Stop!" Then he said something in Romanian. Katie only caught part of what he said. She was concentrating on getting to the souvenir stands in time to buy some things. She wanted to bring her mom and grandma something from where their family had lived. Then, in English, he said, "No. You must get on bus now. You no have time for you to shop."

Just then, sunlight reflected off Katie's necklace. It caught Lupu's attention. As he started to speak, he stumbled on his words even more. "You . . . you . . . you had time already. Get on bus or you can take taxi back to dorms." The expression on his face changed. He looked lost in thought.

Cam wasn't too upset, but he saw Katie was. Her face was turning red. Cam thought Katie didn't like Lupu before, but now she probably couldn't stand him. Trying not to say what was on her mind, she kept her lips closed tightly.

Lupu stuck out his arms and guided them toward the bus and away from the souvenir stalls. He still looked distracted.

Katie sadly gave up trying to get back to the shops. They all started walking to the bus. It was then that John came up with a good idea. He asked, "What are we doing tomorrow?"

His question stopped Katie in her tracks. She looked at John and said, "Nothing is planned. Why are you asking now?"

"We could get a taxi to come back here tomorrow," John said.

"Great idea, dude," Cam said.

"Awesome idea," Katie said with a nod.

John couldn't help turning a little red. He wasn't usually the one of the three who came up with great ideas.

Most all the other students were already on the bus. Ruth, who had walked around Bran with other students from school, sat in the bus with an empty seat next to her. John was happy to sit down next to Ruth. Cam sat next to Katie after she slipped into a row. Katie was glad to sit next to Cam. She was also glad she would come back the next day, but she was still mad at Lupu. What made things worse was when they got to the bus and still had to wait for two other students. They came up to the bus eating a folded-up pastry that smelled really good. Many of the students stared with their mouths open at the pastry, sorry they had missed getting some.

Knowing she would return for souvenirs and seeing if that odd woman would still be there, Katie's mood improved.

BACK TO BRAN

Chapter 15

R uth had heard about the trio going back to Bran the next day. She was ready after breakfast to join them. Katie had asked at the school's office for a taxi to take them back to Bran. The taxi driver was waiting for the group outside the cafeteria.

Katie caught sight of Lupu with his phone out. She couldn't see if he was texting or taking a photo with it, but it did look like he had taken their picture. She didn't like it either way. Again, Deeter's earlier words of caution replayed in Katie's head.

As the taxi drove away, Katie saw Lupu look up at them. He quickly brought his phone to his ear. Katie was sure his call had something to do with them.

Ruth and John enjoyed the ride to Bran. They shared the back seat with Cam.

Cam wasn't as happy about the seating arrangement. He would have liked to be sitting next to Katie, but she sat in the front seat. Since she spoke the most Romanian, they thought it would be best for her to sit near the driver.

Cam looked out the window the whole time. He wanted to give John and Ruth time to talk together. Katie was busy talking with the driver. It turned out this driver also spoke a lot of English. He was happy to be able to practice his English with an American girl.

Cam watched as the mountain road passed by an endless number of dark green fir trees. Most of the time, Cam could only see the thick, brown trunks of the trees. When they finally got out of the car at Bran, Cam was surprised to see how cloudy and gray the sky was. *Does this place ever have a welcoming blue sky?* he thought.

All of the teens were happy to see how little the taxi cost when they split it four ways. "Okay, if you don't mind, I'd like to stop and buy some souvenirs before I get to the castle today," Katie told the others.

"Sure, no problem," was the general response.

Katie picked up some t-shirts for herself and her parents. Cam bought a t-shirt for himself. John and Ruth each bought a vampire mug. The mugs had the face of a vampire with long fangs.

As Katie bent over to look at the t-shirts, her necklace dangled in front of her. It hung in front of her for a few seconds before she stood up. A man in a black coat who was looking at his phone by the stand stepped up.

He pointed to the necklace and said something to Katie the others did not understand. She shook her head and said "*Nu, mulțumesc*. No, thank you. Not for sale." Again, he said something to her and she shook her head no. He stepped away from the stall and into the crowd of shoppers.

Cam asked her what the guy wanted. Katie told him, "I guess he saw my necklace. He wanted to buy it. I told him no. There's no way I'd sell it. It belonged to my great-great-grandma when she lived here in Romania. It was handed down to each daughter until it got to my mom. She loaned it to me for the trip."

"I've never seen you wearing it before," Cam said. "I'm sure I would have remembered seeing you with that jewelry. Not too many girls wear a wolf's head pendant."

"That's because I've never worn it before," Katie replied. "I always wanted to wear it, but my mom wouldn't let me. I guess my mom figures I'm old enough now. She thought it might be lucky for me to wear it. I don't think it's been all that lucky for me, though I'm lucky we got to come back to Bran again."

"Well, let's go then," John said. He had been listening to their conversation.

"Yeah, I still want to see that Torture museum," Cam said. "I figured John is an expert guide for it by now. He's spent a ton of time there," Cam joked.

John returned the joke saying, "Torture museum? Here? I didn't know they had one." He gave Cam a quick grin.

Ruth looked at John and said, "What do you mean? We were there together for quite a while yesterday. I had a lovely time." She had understood he was joking with Cam, but she thought to play her own little joke on him.

"I, ah, was just joking with Cam," John said. He looked a bit nervous. He didn't want Ruth to feel their time together didn't mean anything to him. Then, Ruth chuckled and he realized that Ruth was just joking with him. John was quiet the rest of the way to the castle.

Minutes later, the four friends found themselves going inside Bran Castle. They didn't see the same man from the souvenir stall walking behind them up toward the castle too.

I DO LIKE THAT NECKLACE
Chapter 16

Katie was back in the queen's bedroom. The others were going in and out, looking at the different rooms. Katie was looking over some books on a small table when she sensed someone behind her. She expected to see the woman from the day before when she turned around. But no; standing almost face to face with her was a man in a black jacket. It was the man who wanted her necklace. He wasn't moving, he just stood there. Katie could smell the strong scent of garlic and beer. It bothered her that he was so close. She started to worry. Katie stepped to one side to give herself some room from the man.

He asked again if he could buy it. It bothered Katie. Her friends were not in the room. Here was this grown man with no sense of personal space. He looked kind of rough to Katie. She was too bothered by the man to feel the cool draft of air that blew past her.

"The necklace," he finally demanded in English, "show me the back!" Katie was scared. She felt she had to show it to him, but didn't understand why he wanted to see the back of it. He looked as if he might hurt her if she didn't. She wasn't sure what to do. So, she tightly held on to the pendant where he could see it, but not grab it. She hoped by doing it he would leave her alone.

The pendant felt cool in her shaky hand. She was surprised when he took a quick step toward her. He put one hand on her hand holding the pendant. "I must have it!" he said in little more than a whisper.

"No," Katie repeated.

Then the man grabbed the necklace. He started pulling it from Katie's hand. He twisted it and pulled it from her grasp. His strength surprised her.

Katie was speechless. No one had ever attacked her before.

The man made one quick step backwards. His face twisted. He looked down at the pendant and then dropped it as though it was on fire. A burning pain stung his fingers. Loudly, he said, "*Vrăjitoare!*" It was obvious to Katie the man felt pain from the metal of the necklace. Katie wasn't too surprised that he cursed with a word her grandma taught her at Halloween time, 'witch'.

The man looked down at the necklace on the floor, then looked angrily into Katie's face. She saw the anger in his face change to intense fear as his glance went over her shoulder. His eyes popped open as large as they possibly could. His mouth formed a silent scream. He bolted for the door, leaving the necklace on the floor.

Katie slumped to the floor, numb from the attack. She didn't feel the ice cold draft of air behind her. She also missed seeing the young woman in a pretty blouse fade away.

The man knocked into Cam, John, and Ruth at the doorway and bowled them over. They didn't know what hit them. Katie couldn't even think to turn and find out what the man had seen behind her. All she could do was stare at the necklace on the wooden floor in front of her. It looked different in some way than it had before. The backside of the necklace faced up. She had never thought about the back of it. There was a slight design on the side she could see. There was a letter 'M" and it had a squiggly design above it. She thought it was funny that she had never noticed that before.

Katie stared at the necklace on the floor until she became aware of the sounds her friends were making. She looked up and saw them getting to their feet.

The three started talking at the same time.

"Who was that guy?" John said, louder than he meant to.

"What was going on? Are you okay?" Cam asked Katie, concerned.

"You look like you've seen a ghost," Ruth said.

It was that last statement that woke Katie out of her fog of confusion. She shook her head, looked around the room, stood up, and then turned to her friends.

"Thank you! I'm sooo glad to see you guys!" she said, louder than she expected as she ran to them. She brought them into a big group hug. After she let go of her hold on them, she stepped back and worked on calming herself.

Ruth stepped over and picked up the necklace off the floor. She held it out and asked, "Isn't this yours? Wow, it's freezing."

"Yes. It was the guy from the souvenir stall, the one who wanted to buy my necklace. He tried to steal it! He pried it out of my hand. Then, he got this weird look on his face, dropped it, called me a witch, and then ran."

"That jerk! He could have hurt you," Cam said as he started toward the door to go after the man.

"No, wait Cam!" Katie said. "It's not safe for you to go after him."

Cam wanted to go find the guy, but he could see Katie needed all her friends there. He stepped outside the door, but he couldn't see or hear anyone. He went back inside to Katie and the others.

"That was really bad AND really weird," Katie said as she took Cam's hand and held it in hers for comfort. Her face was pale. "I don't know what made him drop the necklace. All I remember is him looking horrified and then dropping it. Then my legs went weak and I fell to the floor. I guess I kind of blanked out. I remember being really, really cold. Whatever he saw scared him."

"How odd that the necklace was super cold and you said you were super cold," Ruth said to Katie.

"I don't know what was up with that guy wanting your necklace, but an ice cold area in a castle like this makes me think 'ghost'," John said.

"You sure?" asked Cam. "We haven't seen any definite signs of a ghost here."

"You're right. Well, there was that one strange reflection, but I wasn't able to duplicate it," Katie said. "So, we can't be 100% sure. The only thing I am 100% sure of is that I never want to see that creep again."

"About that guy, I agree. About ghosts, I haven't noticed anything," Ruth said.

"Well, I'm just putting it out there," John said.

"Hey, Katie, you still look shaken up. We'd better get you outside, maybe get something to eat and drink," Cam said.

"Yes, my granny always says in situations like this, doing normal things will help you feel normal," Ruth said.

"Wise woman," John said, with a nod. "I'm definitely down for getting something to eat. Anything to take our minds off what happened. Right now, I feel pretty helpless. I'd know what to do at home, but here?"

"I think we all feel that way," Cam said. "Let's find someone we can report the attack to here in the castle. They must have some security people around here who can tell us what we need to do now."

GETTING A BITE
Chapter 17

Reporting the attack took longer than expected. It took about an hour to make the report. Even then, the security people said there wasn't much chance of finding the attacker without a photograph. It turns out the castle was old in many ways. They didn't have any security cameras. The teens left feeling disappointed.

After reporting the attack, Katie and the others went outside and down the hill to get some food. By this time, they were all tired and starving.

Katie's friends were concerned about her. She had gone through a lot that day, but she kept telling them she was fine. She felt if she could be strong for them, it would help her be stronger for herself. Even though she was trying to be brave, she was afraid about running into that guy again. She kept looking at the faces of all the men they passed. They all looked like they could have been that guy, but she knew he was probably far away by now.

Cam and John were on the lookout. They tried to spot the attacker in case he was still around somewhere. Without knowing they were doing it, Cam, John, and Ruth covered

Katie from the sides and back. Cam walked to her left, John to her right, and Ruth behind her. Katie saw that and was thankful for their company. She felt much safer.

The four looked for someplace to buy the folded pancake-like food they saw the day before. The man at the stand called it *clătite*. He told them to pronounce it like kla-tee-tay. It was a soft, thin pancake, folded with different fillings. They could have chocolate, bananas, jellies, or meats inside. The girls wanted theirs with ham and cheese inside. The boys chose chocolate and bananas. They all got cans of soda to drink. Then, they found a bench nearby to sit and eat.

Katie's three friends sat without talking while Katie went over her story again. They all felt better after having had something to eat.

Cam reviewed the day's events in his mind. He was a little troubled. Romania had seemed like a safe place, until now. But he knew bad people can be anywhere. They'd have to be more careful now.

"That is a beautiful necklace you have," Ruth said. "It looks like one-of-a-kind. Where did you get it?" she asked.

Katie didn't want to talk about the necklace. After all, it reminded her of the attack. Since Ruth wasn't there when she told the others about it, she felt she needed to tell Ruth. But, for safekeeping, Katie kept it behind her shirt. "My mom gave it to me. It belonged to my great-great-grandma who lived in Romania 100 years ago."

"And your mom thinks it's lucky?" Cam asked.

"Well, it doesn't seem to be as lucky for me. But my mom thinks it has been lucky for her. She wore it when good things happened to her like when she got into college, and when she met my dad," Katie said. Katie blushed a little when she thought about how that might have sounded. She hoped it didn't sound like she was wearing it to find a boyfriend.

The time talking on the bench helped Katie to calm her nerves and she started to feel more like her normal self.

"I'd like to walk around some more," Katie told the others as she stood up.

"I'll go with you," Cam said. "I'm not going to leave you alone, especially here. That guy might still be around."

"Judging by the look on his face when he ran away, I'm pretty sure he's long gone," Katie said. "But, to be on the safe side, sure."

"Well, where are you going?" asked John. "I'd like to go back and get one of those ham and cheese pancakes. I'm still hungry."

"I think I'll go with John if you don't mind," Ruth said. "I saw some sweets they were selling near the pancakes. They looked quite good."

John and Ruth went back to where they had found the *clătite*. Katie and Cam walked toward a park-like area nearby. As Katie and Cam walked side by side, she felt Cam slip his hand around hers. It did make her happy and a little safer, but the feeling didn't last. The guy attacking her came back into her head. She tried to push thoughts of him out of her mind by thinking of other things.

Katie and Cam followed a small path below the castle. They walked for 15 minutes before coming across a small stone chapel built into the mountainside. They went up the steps to get to the locked iron gates in front of it.

"Oh, wow," Katie said. "That's where the Queen's heart was kept. You know, the one the teacher told us about on the bus."

"I gotta say, that sounded gross. Why did they take her heart out?" Cam asked.

"She wasn't alive when they took it. And, she wanted it to stay in the area she loved. They buried her body in a royal burial ground with a lot of other kings and queens of Romania. I read she loved it here and the people loved her. She was a special person, so they followed her request."

"It still sounds kind of gross, but I guess if you love a place so much . . ." he said.

"She did, from what I read."

Cam pointed to a sign carved out of stone above the chapel. It said, *Aici a fost depusă în anul 1940. Inima Reginei Maria a României.* "What does that mean?" Cam asked.

"It's written in simple Romanian. It says, 'Here was placed in 1940, the heart of Queen Marie of Romania'."

"Wow, there's a lot to learn. Who knew I'd be learning so much history on this trip?" Cam said. "You amaze me sometimes with how much you know."

Without thinking, Katie gave Cam a quick hug. She had been through a tough day and was glad for Cam's company, his compliment, and the hug. As she stepped back from Cam, she glanced over his shoulder and froze.

"Look, Cam, I'm sure that's the guy who attacked me, there, by those trees," she quickly said. She moved her head around, trying to get a better look. Cam turned around too. Just then, the man in the black jacket looked right at them and started to run away.

"You stay here. I'll see if I can see where he goes, and we can tell the police," Cam told Katie as he started to dash off. "Don't worry. I'm just going to follow him," he shouted back to her as he ran.

"No, Cam. That's too dangerous," Katie yelled after Cam. She couldn't think of what to do. She didn't want Cam to catch the guy. She hoped he would just see the guy get into a car and get the license plate number or something like that. *At least Cam's smart enough not to get in a fight with the guy*, Katie thought and hoped she was right.

THE QUEEN'S HEART

Chapter 18

Katie's attention switched from Cam back to her necklace. She felt it getting colder and wondered what would happen next. As she looked up, she turned back toward the chapel and wasn't sure if she was seeing things not really there. The iron gates of the chapel were now wide open. Inside knelt the castle guide in the white, flowy peasant blouse. The woman was praying. Katie couldn't see the woman's face but wanted to ask her who she was. She waited. She was trying to remember how to say what she wanted to ask in Romanian.

A minute passed and the woman was still kneeling. Not wanting to surprise her, Katie decided to make some noise to be sure the woman knew she was there. Katie cleared her throat with a low "ahem" sound. The woman turned toward Katie and smiled.

"*Hallo. Ești bine? Ești bine? Ești bine?*" the woman said. Her voice echoed eerily.

Katie wasn't sure what to say. She wasn't sure if she should be afraid of the woman or not.

"Ah, thank you. Yes, I'm fine. *Sunt bine,*" Katie said, nodding her head. She understood the words, "Hello, are you well?" the woman spoke in Romanian. Katie recognized her from earlier in the castle. *You look pretty solid. You can't be a ghost,* Katie thought to herself.

When the woman didn't say anything, Katie went on. "Thank you for helping me. I'm not sure what that man might have done to me if you weren't there." She realized she was speaking in English, then tried to say the same thing in Romanian. "I wish I could say all that better," Katie added.

"I am a student, *studentă,* going to school here, *aici.* I'm here with my friends. My family, *familia,* used to live around here almost 100 years ago," Katie shared.

"Numele tău de familie este Cristea?" the woman asked.

Katie stood there with a blank look on her face. She understood the woman asked if her family name was Cristea. Words would not come out of Katie's mouth. Finally, she managed to say, "How did you know that? They moved to America a long time ago." Katie saw the confusion on the woman's face. She quickly answered, "*Da!*" (Yes!)

Katie didn't see how the woman could know her great-great-grandma's last name.

How could you know that? Katie thought to herself. Katie was shocked.

Just then, Katie heard Cam yelling to her. She turned around to see where he was. He was jogging through the trees toward her. "That's my friend, Cam," she said as she turned back to the woman.

Katie was confused. The woman was gone and the chapel gates locked shut. It was as if the woman had never been there at all. A chill ran through her. "Where did you go?" she called. "Where did you go?" Katie felt empty. *Was the woman even real?*

"I was chasing that guy. Didn't you hear me when I left?" Cam asked. He felt confused. He was sure Katie heard him as he ran off.

He got closer and saw a look of total confusion painted on Katie's face. She was looking around the chapel and calling inside. But Cam couldn't see anyone other than Katie. He glanced inside. It looked like no one had been inside for years.

He turned to Katie. "Is everything okay? I tried to keep up with that guy, but he had too much of a head start. I'm not sure if he got into a car right away. I couldn't see him anywhere near here," Cam reported.

Katie's first response was, "Yes!" It was immediately followed by, "I mean no! I'm not sure how I am. That woman from the castle was right here. She was praying at the chapel. I started talking to her and she knew my family's name. She knew my great-great grandma's last name. I don't know how she could have known that. It was weird. And when I heard you calling and turned away, she disappeared. She wasn't anywhere, just gone."

Cam wasn't sure what to think. It was hard to believe what Katie was telling him. Did the attack in the castle shake her up more than she had admitted. "First, let's get back to John and Ruth. Then, we'll go back to the dorm and away from here."

Katie was okay with that idea. She needed to leave the weird things that happened in Bran that day. They walked back to the food area and found John and Ruth.

As the teens neared the area where taxis waited, they were surprised to see the taxi driver who brought them standing there. He nodded to them when he saw them and opened the car doors.

This time Cam sat up front next to the driver on the return trip. Katie sat between Ruth and John. She thought she might feel better in the middle, and she could fill them in on what they missed at the chapel. Ruth couldn't believe it, but John believed every word.

Cam felt like the cab driver was too interested in hearing Katie's story. When Cam tried to talk to the driver, the driver didn't seem to understand Cam's English. Cam gave up trying to talk to the man.

DINNER BACK AT THE DORMS
Chapter 19

Katie, Cam, John, and Ruth all felt much better after they returned to their dorm that day. Because they had a few minutes before dinner they went straight to their rooms to put their things down. After that, they walked down to dinner together. Again, without thought, they put Katie in the middle of them as they walked. Katie wasn't sure if the others did it on purpose, but it did help her to relax more.

Dinner was a hearty stew with meat and veggies. Though it wasn't exactly like Katie's mother's stew, she felt it was the next best thing. The others enjoyed it too. Everyone got a bowl of corn mush along with the stew. It's called *mamaliga* in Romanian. On top of each bowl of *mamaliga* was a long, green pepper.

Katie saw Ruth going for the pepper out of the corner of her eye. *Oh, no!* she thought. Katie had experienced hot peppers before. Her mother would serve them, but it only took one bite for Katie to know they were too hot for her.

Ruth hadn't had peppers like these at home. So, when she saw the pepper in front of her, she thought she would give it a try. *They wouldn't give a bunch of students from around the world peppers that are wickedly hot*, she thought. So, without asking anyone else, she picked up the pepper and took a big bite. The tears started streaming from Ruth's eyes the second she closed her mouth on the pepper.

Without hesitation, Katie grabbed the bowl of bread rolls. She thrust it to Ruth.

Cam and John didn't know what was going on. They only saw the tears and then the bowl of rolls. They hadn't seen Ruth take the pepper.

"What's wrong, Ruth? John asked. "Katie, what's wrong with Ruth?"

"She just found out that all peppers are not created equal."

Ruth tore a large piece from the bread roll and stuffed it into her mouth. After some quick chewing, she grabbed her water glass. Katie held up her hand to stop her. "Don't drink the water!" she warned. "It only spreads the heat around your mouth. Soak it up with the bread."

It took a couple of minutes before Ruth stopped eating the bread and could say something. "Oh, my word. That was the hottest thing I've ever eaten. Giving me that bread was brilliant, Katie. Thank you."

"You're welcome. I learned that the hard way, from experience," she said. "My grandma thought it was very funny."

"Yes, travel can be dangerous, but it is educational," using a serious voice, Cam joked.

The rest of the meal was uneventful, which is exactly how they all wanted it to be.

KATIE AND RUTH GET TO TALK
Chapter 20

Katie and Ruth were both in their beds and looking forward to a quiet night. The two girls were surprised to find out they both had pretty much the same night-time routine. They set the next day's clothes out, took their showers, brushed teeth, and got in their pajamas.

Though Katie had to question what Ruth meant when she said, "I do think it's time to put on our *jim jams* and pop into bed."

In a short burst of laughter, Katie had to ask, "What are *jim jams?*"

"They're what you sleep in," Ruth said innocently. "Don't you sleep in *jim jams?*"

"Do you mean, pajamas?" Katie asked.

"Yes, I guess that's what you call them in the states. I suppose you don't use the term *jim jams*, do you?"

"No, can't say I've ever heard it used before. We usually call them pj's."

The two girls laughed and got into their beds.

With the lights out, Katie had that awkward moment, not sure if they were going to talk a little or try to go to sleep. She knew she wouldn't be able to go right to sleep, in spite of her full day.

Ruth was the first to say something. "So, Katie, how well do you know John?"

Katie's eyebrows raised with a knowing look. "Oh, pretty well. We've known each other for about 3 years now. We go to the same school and he's in most of my classes. We've become good friends." Katie hesitated in going further. *And 'we're both into ghosts' doesn't sound like a good thing to tell Ruth yet*, Katie thought. So, Katie just said, "He's a nice guy. Why do you ask?"

Ruth started to get a little embarrassed and hid her face in her sheets a little before answering. "I did have a good time with him today. Did he say anything about me?"

"So you like him?" Katie asked, turning to face Ruth.

"Well, yes, I am a little keen on him," Ruth revealed.

"Don't worry. He's a good guy," Katie said as she returned her head to her pillow.

"And Cam. Do you like Cam?" Ruth asked.

"Yeah, I do," Katie said without hesitation. "We've known each other for about a year. I met him when he was trying to get rid of his ghost."

Ruth moved onto her elbow to face Katie. "Ghost? Did you say ghost?"

"Yes, it's a long story, but, yes, it's cleared up now," Katie said. She gave a long yawn as she pulled her sheets to her chin. "Nite."

Oh, my giddy aunt, a ghost? thought Ruth. It was an expression she used often when she was surprised. It was just one of the odd phrases she picked up from her Granny. She was dying to know more, but she saw Katie was falling asleep. She tried to do the same.

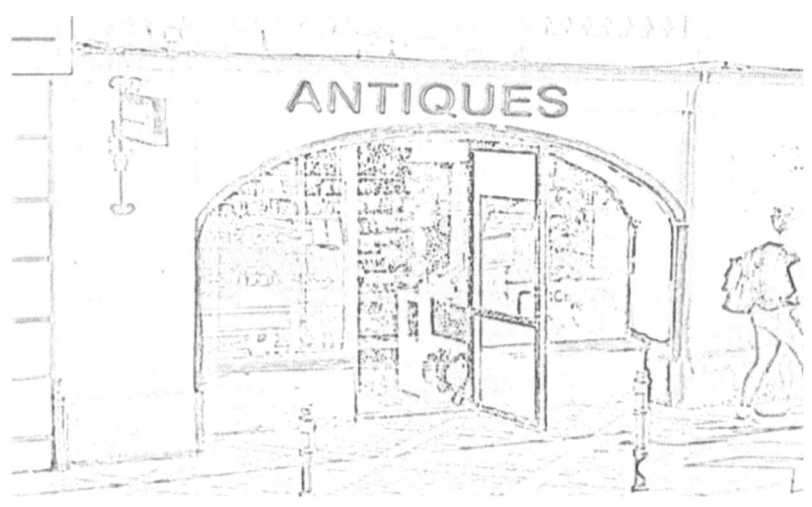

BREAKFAST, SCHOOL, AND A WALK

Chapter 21

"So, in my dream, a ghost came into our room and tried to wake us, but we were too tired to wake up. Then, the ghost waved pancakes in front of us. That's when I woke up." Ruth told Katie.

They both laughed and got ready for the day.

At breakfast, Katie saw Lupu sitting at a nearby table. She felt he was watching her table a lot. She wished she knew why he was watching them. He made her uneasy. Radu was sitting with Lupu. None of the teens could easily describe what Radu actually did at the summer school. It seemed like officially he was a teacher's assistant or maybe a camp counselor. But, to the students, he seemed like someone who was only there to do whatever Lupu told him to do.

Cam and John had been sitting with their backs to Radu and Lupu so they hadn't seen them yet.

After the two left the cafeteria, Katie asked Ruth if she had noticed Lupu watching them. "Yes, and he gives me the creeps."

Katie was glad to get to class that day, though she wished Cam and the others were in her class. The kids in her class were nice, but she didn't know them as well as she knew Cam and John. She knew she could confide in the boys.

Katie was surprised at how well she was able to pay attention to what was going on in class. She thought she might be too distracted from the events of the day before.

After class, Cam met Katie at the door of her room. "Hey, or should I say '*Bună*'?" he asked. He was trying to use a Romanian word he had just learned.

"Either is fine. I'm glad you're learning something," she joked.

"Me too, but it isn't easy. Hey, John and Ruth are out sitting on the lawn, getting some sun," he told her. They walked together to meet up with their friends.

John and Ruth were among several other students who were making their way to the bus going back to the dorm when Katie and Cam caught up with them. Waiting in line to get on the bus, Katie saw Lupu push his way to the front of the line and board the bus. When Katie saw Lupu get on the bus, she didn't feel like sharing it with him.

"Anybody want to walk back to the dorms?" she asked. "It's got to be only about a 20 minute walk. We could check things out better that way."

The others agreed since it was such a nice day.

The path back to the dorms was an easy one to find. They walked the same streets the bus had taken them each day of the previous week. While walking, the general conversation was on how old the city looked. The streets were fairly narrow while the sidewalks were wide. When the streets were made most people walked places and didn't even have a car, unlike in newer American cities. It all made the streets very different from those in the US. "How about for you, Ruth?" John asked. "Do the streets and buildings look this old in England?"

"Oh, not in the bigger cities, though we have got some smaller villages that look positively ancient."

"Even some of the cars here look really old. See this one over there, a *Dacia*," reading the name off the back of the car. "What kind of a car is that?" he asked.

"That's an old Romanian car from the communist days. The name *Dacia* comes from the people who first lived in the country of Romania," Katie told him. "Remember, we talked about that before we came here. Cam and his mom saw a show on it. Cam told us about it."

"Oh, yeah. The Dacians hid a lot of gold so the Romans couldn't get it. It'd still be cool to find a Dacian coin," John said.

"Oh, it's not just gold coins. Some of the gold was big blobs of the stuff. Some was made into jewelry and all kinds of things," Cam said.

"I'll bet somebody already found it and it's stashed away someplace," John said.

"Wouldn't that be brilliant if we were to find some while we're here?" Ruth asked. "But I don't think I'll be going out behind the dorms and dig about, looking for it."

"Yeah, it'd probably be too hard to find a store that sells shovels," Cam joked.

On their walk, they stopped to window shop at different stores along the way. At a clothing store, Ruth ran inside to look at a shirt that was in the window. John and Cam waited for her outside. Katie walked past a few more stores before stopping outside an old antique store. As she looked in through the darkened window, she saw a woman slowly coming from the back of the store toward the window. The woman moved smoothly; it was as if she was gliding. Katie thought the woman must work there until she felt that chill run through her body again. When Katie looked up to make eye contact with her, she saw the saleswoman looking directly into her eyes. It was the woman from Bran Castle. Katie gave a startled jerk backward when she realized it was her.

Katie instinctively glanced for Cam and her friends, then realized that Cam was standing next to her. "That's the woman! That's her!" she told Cam.

When Katie turned back to point to the window, there was no one in it.

Before Cam could ask, "Who's where?" Katie looked through the glass again, before bolting inside. Cam was right behind her. The antique store sold a variety of old things, mostly jewelry. There, in the back corner of the store stood a man. He was cleaning a display case. He looked up and then turned away when he saw Katie. "*Buna ziua*," he said, keeping most of his face looking down at the case while he worked. Katie didn't notice that the man didn't look up at her.

"The woman who was just here. Where did she go?" Katie asked, too excited to ask in Romanian.

The salesman was confused. He shook his head. In English, he said, "Please, speak slowly."

In a slow, drawn-out voice, Katie said, "Where did the woman who was in here go?"

The man shook his head and said, "No woman here. Only me. For one hour."

A quick shiver went up Katie's spine. "That's weird. I know I saw a woman in here from the street. You saw her, didn't you Cam?"

"No, I didn't see anyone. Are you sure you saw her in here?" he asked. "It wasn't just a reflection from outside?"

"Yes. I'm sure of it. She was looking right at me."

The two thanked the salesman and walked out of the store. The man never did turn to look at them. As they left, the salesman went into a back room and pulled out his phone. He made a short call and then told his assistant, a young boy, to watch the store. He grabbed his jacket as he left through a back door.

"She's got to be a ghost!" Katie said to Cam.

"But, we're not at the castle now," Cam replied. As they stood in front of the window talking, Ruth and John walked up.

"What's up, Katie? It looks like something's been going on here," John said.

As Katie and Cam started telling John what happened, Ruth stepped over to the store's window and less than a minute later she walked over to Katie and took her arm. "You've got to see this."

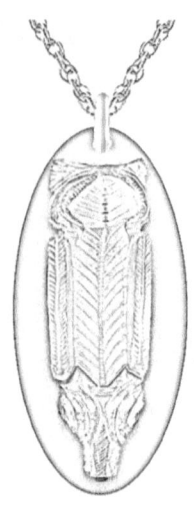

JUST LIKE KATIE'S
Chapter 22

R uth took Katie to the store window. She pointed to some jewelry. "That looks rather like your necklace, doesn't it?" she asked Katie.

Katie stepped closer to get a better look. In the window were a few pieces of jewelry much like Katie's. There were some gold-colored bracelets with a wolf's head on each end. One necklace was a lot like Katies, though not exactly. It had a similar wolf's head on it.

Katie instinctively touched the pendant of her necklace. She could feel its shape. *It is similar*, she thought. *Odd, now it feels cold again.*

Before she could give it any more thought, she looked up into the dark glass in front of her. She observed the reflection of her face next to Ruth's. Between their reflections was the woman's face again. At first, her face looked pleasant. In fact, it kind of looked like Katie's. The scene made Katie flash to a memory of a ride at Disneyland. The woman looked like one of those hitch-hiking ghosts riding in the seat with some unsuspecting person in the Haunted Mansion ride. Katie almost giggled, but she didn't have time. In the next moment, the lady's face changed into something scary. Anger twisted her face.

The change shook Katie. She hadn't seen this side of the woman before. She still thought the woman might be a ghost, but wasn't sure if it would hurt anyone or not.

The young woman's face turned a bright red and then burst into flames before disappearing. As Katie refocused her eyes, a different reflection came into view. Behind the girls, across the street, stood Lupu. Katie called out, "Cam!"

As they watched, a man in a black jacket walked up to Lupu and pointed over his shoulder to the store. Lupu looked at the store and when he saw the students watching him, he waved the man away. Both men walked in two different directions. The teens noted that Lupu turned and walked off in the direction of the dorms.

"That was creepy. How long he was watching us?" Cam asked. "And, that guy. He looked like the salesman from the antique shop, but now with a black jacket on."

"Yeah. What's wrong with that guy?" John asked.

Katie didn't respond to the boys. Her mind was in many places trying to make sense of everything that was happening. *Wait! Was that the same guy who attacked me for the necklace? It looked a lot like him now that I've got a better look at him, but was it? Was the woman in the window mad at me, or at Lupu for being there?*

"Do you think the guy who tried to get the necklace was working with Lupu?" Katie asked.

"I wouldn't be surprised," Cam said as he looked to see if he could see either the man or Lupu. Neither one was in sight anymore.

Bringing the subject back to the jewelry, Katie asked, "Do you think there's a connection between my necklace and the jewelry in this store? They seem to be rare designs. I mean, it makes sense to see something like it here, in Romania. I'd never seen anything like my necklace at home before. That jewelry is similar, and there is one piece that looks pretty close," Katie told Ruth.

"I've got it! If someone is going to take your necklace, maybe you need them to take one you don't care about," Ruth said.

Katie took only a second to think about it. She looked inside and saw a young clerk there. Since the man wasn't there now, she said, "Let's go back inside."

In the store, Katie found out the jewelry was not old. It only looked like Dacian jewelry. There were two big differences between Katie's necklace and the one in the store. One difference was that the jewelry in the store wasn't real gold. It was only gold plated. The other difference Katie saw when she turned the pendant over. The store's necklaces didn't have the symbol on the back as hers did.

She bought the necklace and put her own necklace in the protective pouch that came with the new one. She then put the pouch in her pocket for safekeeping. She put the new necklace around her neck.

"Why'd you buy another necklace that looks like yours?" asked John.

Ruth jumped in and said, "This way, if someone pinches this necklace off her neck, they'll get the phony one."

Cam and John both nodded in agreement. Then they decided they were hungry and hurried along their way to get lunch.

As one large group, all the summer school students went on a field trip after lunch. They walked to an art museum not far from the dorms. At the museum, Katie and Cam stayed together with the main group of students. Ruth and John wandered off.

After dinner at the dorms, followed by a short walk into town, the teens were ready for a quiet night's sleep, but things don't always go as planned . . .

UNINVITED GUEST
Chapter 23

K atie had gone through her nighttime routine long before Ruth arrived. Ruth had stayed downstairs talking to John. So, when she came into their room, Katie was already in bed but barely awake.

"I'll just be a sec," Ruth said, as she picked up her things and headed to the bathrooms down the hall.

"Ok," Katie said sleepily. "I might not be awake when you get back." A long yawn followed her words and she turned to face the wall.

Katie was nearly asleep when her heart started pounding. She could even feel the beating in her head. She started to worry. She had only felt her heart beat as hard when she had been running in her P.E. class at school.

The door opened, shut, and then she heard the squeak of Ruth's bed-frame. Katie heard the question, "Tired?" Ruth's British accent seemed to be thicker than usual.

"Yes. Every day is long here," Katie mumbled, thinking more about her pounding heart than what Ruth had said.

"So, your relative who originally brought your necklace to America, what was her name?"

"Anna Cristea. She was my great-great-grandma. No one knows all that much about her. Why do you ask?"

"Yes, Anna. Your great-great-grandmother was a lovely woman and a very good friend."

Still facing the wall, Katie opened her eyes. Something wasn't right. Though similar, this voice was not Ruth's. Katie was wide awake now. She rolled over to make sure it was Ruth she was talking to. As she rolled enough to face Ruth's bed, the door opened and Ruth walked into the room. Katie snapped her head toward the opening door. Katie's gaze darted between Ruth at the door and the empty bed.

"Wait! Did you just get here?" Katie said. She pushed herself up as she spoke.

"Yes, I was down in the lav, like I said. I thought I'd better nip in and take a quick shower," Ruth said. "Were you just talking to yourself as I was coming in? It sounded that way to me."

"I was talking to you!" Katie said, sounding confused.

Ruth put her things down and said, "What do you mean? I just got here. You saw me come into the room."

Katie leaned back against the wall and pulled her knees up to her chest. She kept her arms around her legs. She didn't say anything for a few seconds. She had to process what just happened. She quickly came to an unlikely conclusion, but she didn't have any other explanation for it.

"I must have been talking to *two* ghosts in Bran. Now don't freak out on me. I'm pretty sure the woman I've been seeing is a ghost. She's never spoken in English though. This last one was different. She sounded older and spoke with an accent more like yours. I thought I was talking to you."

Ruth showed no reaction to what Katie had said. Her only reply was, "Oh, how lovely." Katie wasn't sure if she was more surprised at the idea of ghosts or Ruth's strange reaction.

"You heard me, right?" Katie asked. "Ghosts?"

"Oh yes. Back home in England, we hear of them all the time. You do believe these are friendly ghosts, don't you?" Ruth asked.

"I'm not sure. They've been nice enough to me, but I saw a scary side of the one today in the store window. And there was that time at the castle with that creep who tried to take my necklace."

"What did this one want?" Ruth asked as calmly as if she were asking what time they should get up the next morning.

"She asked about my great-great-grandma whose necklace I have. The ghost must have known her." She moved to the edge of the bed with her feet hanging over, facing Ruth. "She said my great-great-grandma was nice and a good friend."

"So, your great-great-granny was friends with the ghost? Perhaps that's why neither John, Cam, nor I have seen her."

"Probably," was Katie's response. "Strange. This ghost spoke perfect English. She sounded British, like you." Katie didn't face Ruth as she was talking. She was thinking about what had happened before Ruth came into the room.

"I don't think I know any English ghosts here, and none from my family," Ruth joked.

The two sat in for a minute or two in silence after that not saying anything.

Ruth broke the silence. "So, have you seen other ghosts before?"

"Well, no, not directly. There was Cam's ghost. I never saw him. He just left notes for Cam. Also, there were a couple of other times that John and I could feel the presence of some ghosts, but we didn't talk to them like I've talked with these women."

"Oh, I see. Perhaps they'll drop by again soon. Well, goodnight then," Ruth said.

Ruth fell asleep right away while Katie laid awake. She had too many things going on in her head.

At breakfast the next morning, Katie and Ruth looked around before telling Cam and John about the ghost's visit. They didn't want anyone to hear. "Cam and John will be okay, but in general, people can freak out when it comes to ghosts," Katie had told Ruth earlier.

"Here we go again," Cam said. Cam still remembered how much his ghost had scared him. He made an unhappy face. Katie ignored him. She knew he'd be ok with it in time.

"No, it's different with this one," Katie said. "They're scary, but in a friendlier way. I know that doesn't sound right, but that's how they seem to me. They haven't even shown themselves to you or John. I need you to trust me on this."

Cam knew he had no choice. All he could say was, "Okay, what next?"

"Thanks. So, this ghost might be someone who knew my great-great-grandma. Maybe someone she went to school with?"

"Could be," John said, trying to be helpful. *I wonder if there's a school for ghosts*, John joked to himself.

YOU FOUND SOME GOLD?
Chapter 24

I t wasn't long before Radu stopped at Katie's table. Radu patted Cam on the shoulder as if they were longtime friends.

"I'm Radu. You probably know that already. How are you all doing? Any problems?" Radu asked. While he was asking this, he didn't take his eyes off of Katie, staring at her necklace most of the time. The whole time he was there, the necklace in Katie's pocket was getting colder.

"So, the records show only one of you has a Romanian family background, yes?" he asked.

"Yes," Katie answered, "it was a very, very long time ago that my great-great-grandma lived around here. She's actually buried in Bran. That was around 1940." When she said that, the necklace got cold. It started to make Katie shift around in her chair.

"Yes, Hungary controlled much of Romania before World War II. But, of course, it has always belonged to Romania. The Romanians are direct descendants of the Dacians. The Dacians owned all of Northern Romania long before the Hungarians," Radu said in a self-important kind of way.

"Yes, we heard that," John told him. "We heard the Dacians had lots and lots of gold they hid from the Romans." John was trying to impress Radu with his knowledge of the Dacians. "We're going to be looking. Don't be surprised when I tell you we found some."

Radu couldn't believe his ears. Unfortunately, he didn't understand John's words correctly. He thought John told him they found some of the famous Dacian gold. He knew they were going places after school; except he didn't know where. But, to make sure he understood correctly, Radu asked John, "You found some gold?"

Ruth thought Radu was joking so she joked back, "Oh, yes. It was brilliant. They can't carry it all, they have too much."

Radu's eyes lit up. He took one last look at Katie's necklace. "I must leave. I have to correct a problem for others in the group." He turned and headed straight for the door before the teens could tell him they had not really found any gold.

"Why did you tell him that, Ruth?" Katie asked. "Now he thinks we found the gold."

"Nonsense, he does not think that," Ruth said and then paused. "Oh, dear. You might be right," she said.

Cam said, "Well, it doesn't matter. I don't mind playing a little joke on him. Let him believe we've found tons of gold. He's always with that creepy Lupu. I don't like or trust either one of them. Let them run around to see if we have it."

COLLYWOBBLED
Chapter 25

After two weeks of class, the four students were happy to be making some progress in learning the language. They learned a lot of Romanian words and were able to use them in simple sentences. John even asked his teacher how to order *clătite*. He'd be ready next time he found some.

Getting back to the dorms after school, the girls decided to eat before going up to their rooms. The boys offered to save the girls the long walk up the stairs to their room. "We'll be nice and take your books upstairs for you," Cam said. "We'll drop them off in our room and you can get them after lunch."

The girls waited outside the cafeteria for the boys to return. They had planned to sit at the same table. To do that, all four of them had to go inside at the same time. If they didn't, the lunch ladies made students sit at different tables in order to fill them up. The ladies wanted the least number of tables to get dirty. The two girls talked while they waited.

The boys came down within five minutes, and they all walked into the cafeteria together. Lunch was delicious like all their meals had been. Ruth and John took over most of the conversation during lunch. The two described their homes and schools. They enjoyed learning about each other's lives.

Cam suggested they take a walk into town after lunch. Before they did that, Katie and Ruth wanted to go back to their room to use the bathroom and get their books from the boys.

Everyone went to the boys' room first. Remembering they left their room a mess, John went ahead to get there first. He remembered what his mom told him before he left home, "Keep your dorm room picked up." He didn't want Ruth to see his messy room. He came out of the door just as the others reached his room.

"Here you go," he said. Ruth tried to take a peek inside, but John did a good job of keeping the door closed.

When they got to the girls' room, Katie said, "Please wait here." She wanted to make sure there wasn't anything private left out in their room.

"Oh, my gosh!" Katie said.

"Who did this?" Ruth said as she gaped at the messy room. "This isn't how we left it this morning!"

The room was a mess. Someone had pulled the mattresses from the beds. The girls' bags were open on the floor and their things were tossed all around the room.

"Someone's trashed our room!" Katie said. She felt embarrassed and mad. The thought of someone going through all her clothes was awful.

John's face turned red with anger. "I don't know who did this, but if I ever get my hands on them . . ." his voice faded without finishing his sentence.

"We'd better go down and tell someone in the office. They need to know," Cam said.

"For sure," Katie agreed. "John, could you stay here with Ruth? I need to go in case we don't find someone who speaks English, but I don't want to go alone. Maybe, Cam, could you come with me?"

"Sure." both Cam and John said at the same time.

It was a few minutes later when Radu came up the stairs with Cam and Katie. John couldn't quite understand why Radu came until he remembered Radu was the guy they were supposed to bring their problems to. John didn't think Radu would be able to help much.

The first thing Radu asked was if they had locked the door. "Of course we did. I remember locking it," Katie told him.

Standing outside the room, he looked in and asked, "Did you see if anything was stolen?"

"I don't believe anything was stolen from me," Ruth said.

"Same here," Katie said.

When the girls didn't go inside their room, Radu was visibly disappointed. "Maybe you should go in and look, just to be sure."

Neither Katie nor Ruth wanted to go into their room at this point. Radu again insisted, "Make sure you look wherever you would have hidden anything." This sounded odd to Katie. So, she lied and said, "Actually, we did that before we went to get you."

Radu looked disappointed. Reluctantly, he said, "Oh, okay. I will file a report with the office. You will have to sign it later."

"That's fine," Katie said. All eyes were on Radu as he left the hallway and started down the stairs.

"What was that about?" Cam asked. "You didn't have time to look through your things."

"First of all, I don't have anything hidden. Secondly, I didn't like the way Radu wanted me to show him where I might hide something."

"Yeah, good thinking," John said.

"I'll bet it was Radu or Lupu who did this," Katie said, "Or maybe Lupu's friend in the black jacket?"

"I should think it was Lupu," Ruth said.

"I agree," said Cam. "Radu did spend some time talking to us at breakfast. He never has before."

John walked up to Katie and asked, "Do you think maybe it could be *poltergeists*?"

"That's possible, but Lupu and Radu are more likely the guys who did it. The ghosts I've seen haven't done anything nasty to me."

Cam and John stood in the hallway while Katie and Ruth went back into their rooms to straighten things up. Later, John and Cam helped the girls flip the mattresses back into place.

Cam said, "Do you girls want to switch rooms?"

"Thank you, Cam. I was hoping you'd ask, but I didn't want to make you guys move," Katie said. "I don't think I can sleep in this room after what happened."

"That would be quite a fave if you did that for us," Ruth said. "This room's got me *collywobbled*," she added.

The three Americans burst out laughing. "*Collywobbled*!? What does that mean?" Katie asked. "We've never heard that expression before." Ruth's British slang broke the gloomy mood.

"Oh, it means '*kind of sick*', like '*sick to my stomach*' kind of sick. I've never had someone break into my room before."

"Don't worry," John said, "it'll only take a minute or two to swap rooms."

Five minutes later, the boys had their bags in the hallway and the swap began. Katie wanted to change the bedding too; it took about 20 minutes in all. "I'm sure no one will care about the swap," Cam said.

"Thanks, I am a lot better now, Cam," Katie said. She put her hand in her pocket and felt her necklace safely in its pouch. She noted that it wasn't cold at all now.

A REGAL GUEST
Chapter 26

It had been a disturbing day for both Katie and Ruth. The girls were finally starting to settle into their new dorm room. They had gotten ready for bed and were talking before lights out.

"Do you think they were trying to find something in particular in our room?" Ruth asked.

"I'm not sure, but it's a good guess. And my guess would be they were looking for my necklace, in case I had left it in the room. I bet it was Lupu. Did you see today how Radu was staring at my necklace? I bet he'd be surprised to find out it's in my pocket. I'm not taking any chances by leaving it in the room, or even wearing it where someone could grab it and run."

"Good idea. Definitely sounds like something I would expect either one of them to do," Ruth replied. "I hope it's not bad timing, but could I see your necklace? I never really got a good look at it," Ruth said.

"Sure." Katie took the necklace out of the pocket of the jeans she had set aside to wear tomorrow. She opened the pouch it was in and handed it to Ruth. Ruth held it up to take a better look.

"Lovely," she said, "but, in a powerful way."

"Try it on. Go ahead. See how it looks on you," Katie told her friend.

Ruth became tense with worry about anything happening to Katie's necklace while she had it on. "You sure?" she asked.

"Sure," Katie said.

Ruth put the necklace on and smoothed it out. She went over to the mirror on the wall above the small sink to take a look. It only took a few seconds before a cold draft of air flooded the room. The small hairs on Ruth's arms stiffened. Ruth gave a sharp, high pitched scream. The room plunged into darkness. Katie screamed out of surprise. A gust of wind blew open the windows.

Ruth spun around in the dark to turn away from the mirror. By the time she finished turning, the lights came back on. The window curtains were flapping through the open windows. Her attention went to Katie who was jumping up from her bed.

The two girls rushed to meet each other in the middle of the room. Katie twisted her head around as best as she could while trying to hold onto Ruth. Katie tried to see what could have caused the lights to go out and the windows to blow open.

"What happened?" Katie asked. "Are you all right?"

The color had drained from Ruth's face. She wouldn't turn to face the mirror. She couldn't. She stood there holding onto Katie, her face buried into Katie's shoulder.

Ruth pointed to the mirror and said, "There were two faces in the mirror. Two ghosts. One was a young woman's face! She had thick dark hair. She was standing right behind me. It got cold. I'm surprised I couldn't feel her breathing, she was that close. My heart started beating hard. There was also an older woman standing next to her. Their faces looked mad. I didn't know ghosts could look so mean."

"Wait a minute," Katie said. "A young, dark-haired girl and an older woman? One of them sounds like the one I saw before. I never saw the second woman, I only heard her voice."

"And, and I'm pretty sure the other ghost is Queen Marie. She looked exactly as she did in her picture in the castle," Ruth was able to say.

Katie didn't know quite what to say for a second. "Are you sure? The queen? Here? How'd that happen?"

"Well, she did look a lot friendlier in that photo than in person. Maybe it was the state of our room? We're going to need to keep this room a lot cleaner if we're going to entertain royalty," Ruth joked. Even she couldn't figure out how she was able to joke at a time like this.

Katie looked down, waved her head from side to side, chuckled, and said, "Too soon." Then she gave a short burst of laughter.

"I just got a crazy idea," Katie said. Before she could share it with Ruth, there was a sharp knock on their door. Both girls jumped. Katie went to the door but didn't open it. "Yes, who is it?"

"It's me, Cam. Did you girls scream?" he asked with concern in his voice.

Katie opened the door a crack. There in the hallway stood Cam in his gym shorts and a t-shirt. He obviously was ready for bed. There were some other kids out in the hall. They were talking among themselves. A few were trying to peek into Katie's room to see what was going on.

"It's all right. Ruth thought she saw a mouse on the window ledge. We shut the window so we'll be okay now," she said loud enough for everyone to hear.

A girl further down the hallway said, "We'd better close our windows too!" and they ran back to their rooms.

"Really?" asked Cam. He looked relieved.

"No!" Katie whispered. "We saw two ghosts and the power went out in our room. I didn't want to tell everyone that. We're okay now. There's probably nothing for us to worry about right now. We can talk more in the morning. Oh, yeah, except one of the ghosts was Queen Marie."

"Sure," Cam said, keeping his voice low too. "Wait, what, who?"

Now Katie noticed John standing closely behind Cam who was dressed in his gym shorts and a black t-shirt. Cam turned and pushed John slightly to get him moving back to their room. "They're okay. Goin' to tell us about it in the morning. I've got something to tell you back in our room though. Let's get back to bed."

"Do we need to close our windows, too?" asked John. Cam gave him another slight push toward their room.

After closing their door, the girls sat on their beds facing each other. Ruth studied Katie's face for a few moments. "Katie, I didn't have a chance to tell you, but the dark-haired ghost? She looked a lot like you."

"I hadn't noticed it before, though now that you say it, yeah. Maybe you're right. In the back of my mind, I've always thought there was something familiar about her. Familiar, *familia*. Oh, my gosh! I can hardly believe it. Could she be my great-great-grandma, here with me? Is it possible?"

A GHOSTLY VOICE IN THE NIGHT
Chapter 27

"I must be wrong, but . . ." Katie opened the photos on her phone. She scrolled through hundreds of photos before stopping on one. Katie held up the phone to Ruth. Ruth gasped and put her hand to her mouth. On the phone was an old, slightly blurry black and white photo of one of the ghosts.

"That looks like her! How did you ever get a photo of that ghost?" Ruth asked.

"I wasn't sure. I just had a hunch. That's my great-great-grandma, Anna Cristea. That was a photo taken after she arrived in the US back in the 1930s. She looks older in this photo than the ghost, but it could be her." A quick shiver ran up Katie's back.

Ruth looked to Katie. "Have you ever seen your great-great-grandma before? She didn't look as happy when I saw her. She looked quite mad. The older woman didn't look happy either. They both had reddish, glowing eyes."

"That's weird. I know she's dead and all, but I can't imagine she'd be mad at us for anything. I mean, I'm even here in her old country. I'd think she'd be happy I made the effort to come here," Katie said.

"I'd say she should be pleased you came, except, I was the one wearing her old necklace. Perhaps she was upset that I was wearing it. After all, it is yours, and not mine."

"You have a point there. It's like she's one with the necklace. I'm going to try something. Give me the necklace. I'm going to put it on and check it out in the mirror." Ruth was glad to get rid of the necklace. She had already removed it and was holding it out to Katie. Katie put it on over her head and walked to the mirror.

"Nothing. I only see me in the mirror." Katie kept looking at herself for a minute or two before going back to her bed. "I don't get it. I have no idea what causes these ghosts to appear and disappear.

Katie went over to her bed and sat down. Ruth was already lying down in hers. They talked some more about what happened. As they talked, Katie turned and stretched out on her bed. Katie could tell that Ruth was falling asleep. Her speech slowed until she stopped mid-sentence. Ruth fell into a deep sleep. Katie laid there, holding onto the necklace and going over everything that had happened just minutes ago. She could hardly believe it.

Her eyes started to tear up when she realized she had seen and talked with her great-great-grandma. *If only grandma and mom could be here now*, she thought. Her eyes closed and Katie fell asleep, still holding onto the necklace.

The two girls slept soundly. Around two a.m., Katie was paid a visit. If Ruth had been awake, she might have seen a cool fog slowly covering Katie's bed. Ruth might have also seen a woman standing over Katie. The woman looked down at the sleeping girl with a loving look.

"*Dragă* Katie. I am happy you came to me," the ghost said in Romanian, echoing her words.

The ghost tried to stroke Katie's forehead. Katie stirred a little in her sleep. Still asleep, she pulled her blanket up. She felt a little cold.

In Romanian, the ghost added, "There is something for your family at Bran. It is from the Queen. You must go there. There is more you need to know."

The coldness in the room finally woke Ruth. When Ruth opened her eyes, she saw the figure and the cool mist above Katie. Only after a few moments did Ruth wake up enough to understand what she was seeing. Ruth gave a startled cry; her head still half sunk into her pillow. Fortunately, students in the other rooms didn't hear Ruth's half muffled cry. Unfortunately for Katie, she heard it and woke up a bit startled.

Katie sat upright. She shook her head as she looked around the room. Her eyes fell upon Ruth who was holding her pillow out like a shield. There was enough light coming in through the window for them to see each other.

"What happened? Why did you scream? Did you see the ghosts again?" she asked without waiting for answers.

"Yes. Yes, I did," Ruth answered. "This time a ghost was over you. Talking to you. It was the younger one that looks rather like you," Ruth added.

"What'd she say?" Katie asked anxiously.

"I don't know," Ruth said. Katie's shoulders slumped.

"She said it all in Romanian. I couldn't understand her and I probably didn't hear all of it since I was mostly asleep."

"You didn't catch any of it?" Katie asked.

"Give me a moment." After giving it some more thought, Ruth remembered something. "Yes, I do remember hearing the word Bran; obviously the castle, right? Come to think of it, it is the name of a whole town. No, I'm pretty sure she meant Bran Castle. I can't recall any other words she said to you. Sorry."

"I wish she had told me when I was awake. I might not have understood it all, but I might have figured out at least some of what she wanted me to know."

"Wait a minute. I just remembered. She did say something else. I believe she said, 'de la regină', from the Queen'. That I'm pretty sure can't mean anything else."

Neither girl spoke after they went back to bed. Sleep was slow in coming and their minds raced.

WAS HE LISTENING?

Chapter 28

The four teens met in the hallway on their way to breakfast the next morning. Right away Katie told Cam and John about her nighttime visitor. Katie and Ruth had already decided it was easiest to call the younger ghost by her suspected first name, Anna. "So, the words Katie understood Anna saying were 'from the Queen' and 'Bran Castle'."

"Whoa, what if the queen has tons of gold she wants you to find?" John said.

"How did you get all that from what Ruth said?" Katie asked John.

"It's like I said before we came. That castle has tons of gold . . ." John started to say, but a noise from someone moving in the lobby stopped him before he could finish.

Katie just realized how well sound carried in the stairway. They got to the bottom of the stairs in time to see Radu going out the lobby door.

"I wonder if he heard what you were saying." Ruth said, in a low tone.

In the cafeteria, Katie and the others sat down at the first table they came to. John just happened to look around the room to see who was there. He saw Radu and Lupu talking a few tables away.

"They're talking about us," John said, "based on how they keep looking over here."

"Yes, I'm afraid Radu must have heard what was said on the stairs. I don't know if he heard 'from the queen' or 'Bran Castle', but he must have heard John saying there was gold in the castle."

"We're going to have to go back there," Cam said. "Maybe the ghost will come and talk to you there again."

"I hope so," Katie said. "But John, I can't imagine money was left for my family from the Queen. Probably just some pictures or a book or something. I would have heard if my family knew the Queen. That's not something someone would keep a secret."

"You never know," John said as the four students left the cafeteria on their way to the bus.

For Katie, time in class crawled along that morning. John's comment about the gold kept popping back into her thoughts. She kept looking at the clock. While in the other room, John kept asking Cam what time it was.

It seemed like forever before the students finished school for the day and returned to the dorms. Katie and Ruth were happy to see that their room, along with Cam and John's room, was just as they had left them. Cam thought to himself, *I'm not sure our room is any neater than the girls' room after someone broke into it. Maybe we'd better work on that.*

The teens went down to eat lunch. They had asked for a taxi to meet them afterward. They were beyond surprised when they found the same taxi driver from the previous day waiting for them. Katie thought it odd that they kept getting the same driver. After all, there were hundreds of taxis in the town, yet this driver had been available each time they needed one. Something wasn't right.

Katie and the others got into the cab, and 30 minutes later they were walking up the steps to Bran Castle.

SEARCHING FOR... WHAT EXACTLY?
Chapter 29

K atie was glad to be at Bran and out of the taxi. She shared her suspicions with her friends about the driver. The others thought it was odd too.

"Hey, did you see the sign that said there was a special event at the castle tonight and it's closing early today? We'd better get going. We don't have as much time as we thought we'd have." Cam pointed out.

"We'd better split up into two groups. Ruth, you go with John and I'll go with Cam," Katie said. "That way we'll cover more ground in less time."

Everyone agreed to Katie's plan. "I wish we knew what we were looking for exactly," John said.

"Believe me, I do too," Katie said. "All we know is to be here and look for something that a ghost told us about in my sleep. That's not too vague, is it?" she joked.

"Make sure to look at all the pictures and read what's written. Maybe Anna's name will be on something. So, Cam and I will start at the top and work our way down. Ruth and John, why don't you start at the bottom and work your way up? We'll meet in the middle."

Ruth and John went to the old well in the courtyard first. A sign next to the well said Queen Marie put an elevator inside the well shaft back in the 1930s. They looked down into it. The well was only a few feet deep. Someone must have sealed it up. They guessed workers would have found anything hidden there. They went on to the torture museum next.

Katie and Cam climbed the stairs to the top of the castle. Katie suggested they should split up but stay on the same floor. This made Cam a little nervous, but he knew that's what they needed to do. They didn't know what to look for, but they'd try their best. *Ok, let's get this done. We'll find it and that'll finish it,* Cam thought.

Once up in the Queen's bedroom, Katie started looking in earnest. Next to the queen's bed was the window that the ghost had pointed out from. Perhaps the ghost would appear again over there. She was right. Only moments after she stopped at the window to look out, things started to happen.

First, she saw her breath flowing towards the window. As her breath hit the window, it fogged the glass.

Then, reflected on the fogged glass, Katie saw herself and the inside of the room. The thought, *I should have brought a jacket,* jumped into her head. She realized she was cold and the room was now dark. What she saw looked like a different room entirely. It had all changed drastically.

She took her time turning back into the darkened room. It was like someone turned out the lights. It was completely different. From one of the shadows, Anna stepped out. Anna walked slowly toward Katie. Anna had a smile on her face. Katie hoped it would stay there.

"*Dragă, ai venit*! *ai venit, ai venit*." Katie understood 'Dear, you came'. Katie's grandma has said that to her before. *Great so far*, she thought.

Anna said the same thing a few times, "*Dragă, ai venit. Dragă, ai venit*." Katie's emotions were torn. She was glad to see her relative, but she had seen Anna's dark side at the store, and now Anna only spoke in echoing words. It started to scare Katie.

This woman was like a broken record. Katie was relieved when Anna said something else. She said, "*Tu ai colierul meu. Tu ai colierul meu. Tu ai colierul meu*." Why was this woman only echoing short phrases? And, Katie misunderstood part of what Anna said, "You have to find my . . ." What? What did I have to find of hers? What is it? What does *colierul* mean?

Then, Anna said, "Aurul ta-e aici! Aurul ta-e aici! Aurul ta-e aici! Aur de la regina Marie, Aur de la regina Marie, Aur de la regina Marie."

Before Anna could say more, Katie felt the room start to spin. She could see Anna fading away and the room became brighter. When the spinning stopped, Katie was alone in the room, except for Cam standing by the door. The light was behind him and Katie's head was still spinning.

"The gold is here? Gold from Queen Marie?" Katie translated out loud. "The gold is here!" Katie said it more to herself than to Cam. "And, she said I have to find her 'colierul'. What is a 'colierul'?

As her head cleared, she could hear him say, "She . . . she said you have her necklace." His voice was slow and showed his disbelief in what he was translating. He looked stunned and he certainly wasn't Cam!

Who is that!? she thought as she suddenly understood it wasn't Cam at the door. It was the taxi driver.

After it hit him as to what he had told her, he turned and ran out of the room. On his way out, he bumped into Cam and knocked him down.

Cam only saw who ran into him at the last moment. "That was the taxi driver!" he called out.

"Yes, it was. And, I just told him there's gold here in the castle."

As Cam got himself up, he asked, "Did you tell him where it is? Where is it, anyway?"

"Well, it's a good news, bad news thing. The good news is he doesn't know where it is. The bad news is I don't know either. He came in before the ghost could tell me more. I thought he was you. My head was spinning. It's still spinning."

HIGHS AND LOWS
Chapter 30

"Cam, go outside and don't let anyone in for a few minutes. Maybe if no one else is here, I can talk to Anna again."

Katie went back to the window after Cam stepped out of the room. She held her pendant tightly in her hands and closed her eyes. She tried doing that for about five minutes. "Come on, come on," she repeated, though nothing happened. "It's no use," she called to Cam. "I don't know what the difference is now, but it's not working. What if it never works again?"

Katie started to worry. It wasn't the gold that bothered her. To her, the real treasure was this new found connection to her past. A feeling of defeat came over Katie.

She was tired and struggled with her thoughts. *On the one hand, I've met the ghost of my great-great-grandma and even found out that she was friends with a queen. That's a great start in learning more about my family, but my mom and grandma never lived here. Even my great-grandma was just a little girl then. She couldn't remember much about her mother or Romania. But really, I'm not any more Romanian than I was before I came here. No matter what grandma told me before I left home, am I really Romanian at all?*

It was getting late. The castle was starting to close. A security guard walked into the room where Cam and Katie were standing. "*Ne pare rău, dar trebuie să pleci. Este ora* închiderii. Sorry. It is closing time." The guard didn't wait for the couple to leave before he went to other rooms.

Katie's face and even her body language showed her disappointment. Cam gave Katie's hand a squeeze and he smiled at her.

Cam's gesture gave Katie the support she needed. *I'll have to try something new*, she thought as she and Cam walked out of the room. As they got into the hall, they noticed the guard only glanced in each room. It gave Katie a somewhat desperate idea.

She would wait until they were outside the castle before talking about it. First, they had to find John and Ruth.

Cam saw that Katie was slow to leave the castle. She walked extra slowly down the stairs. Ruth spotted Katie and Cam between the second and third floors. "John, here they come now," she said.

"Any luck?" John asked. But, from the expressions on Katie and Cam's faces, he could tell they didn't have much.

"Well, yes and no," Cam said.

"I did find out Anna was going to get some money, gold, from the Queen herself. They were friends. Before she could tell me more, she vanished."

"Well, that sounds good," John said.

"No, it's not good because someone else heard the news. It was the taxi driver. The way he took off after hearing it, I'd say he'll be looking for it too; probably with Lupu," Katie said.

"But, if you don't know where it is, they don't know where it is either," added Ruth.

"True. At least that gives us some time," Katie said.

A MEETING IN THE DARK
Chapter 31

When the teens got to the taxi area outside the grounds of the castle, they found there were no taxis there. Katie was glad there were no taxis there because she didn't want to get the same driver. She no longer trusted that driver. They decided to take the bus back to Brașov. Luckily, there was a bus stop across the street from the taxi station. It was only a 15 minute wait before the bus came along. Everyone bought their tickets from an old woman working in a small booth at the end of the bus stop. They were surprised the bus would only take about 15 minutes longer than the taxi to get to Brașov. Also, it only cost each of them less than four lei of Romanian money, less than one US dollar. Only two other people rode that bus back into town, so the teens had the bus almost all to themselves. It allowed the teens to talk privately.

"I have to try to reach Anna again. This time, alone," Katie told the others.

"Good idea. Let's hope it works," John said.

Their bus ride ended at the Brașov bus station just five blocks from the dorms. They were glad the walk would be short. It had been a long day. The path to the dorms put them on different streets than they had been on before, but they had a good idea of how to get back to the dorms.

In the stores and homes along the way, people were starting to turn on their lights. Some sections of the sidewalks were dark. The teens stepped into one of the darker areas when they saw a taxi parked on the street. They stopped. Luckily, the driver hadn't seen them. The taxi's windows were open, and they saw that it was their taxi driver. He was sitting in his taxi, and he had another person sitting inside, too.

Katie was the first one to spot the passenger. It was Lupu. He and the taxi driver were talking. They must have felt it was safe enough to talk on this quiet street.

While hiding in the shadows, Katie strained to hear what the men were saying. She couldn't understand all the words they used. It sounded like the driver was telling Lupu what he had heard at the castle. She thought she heard that Lupu would go with the driver for the gold tomorrow.

Katie was happy the driver didn't have the gold already. Better still, it sounded like he didn't know where the gold was in the castle.

The taxi didn't stay there for long. Lupu got out of the car and started walking toward the dorm. The taxi drove down a side street farther along the road.

Katie and the others waited a few minutes before going on to their dorm. They wanted to give Lupu enough time. They didn't want to run into him on the street.

That night, in their rooms, Katie and Ruth talked.

"I need to find that gold before Lupu does," Katie said.

"Are you quite sure it isn't going to be dangerous? Lupu doesn't look like someone to go up against. After all, he was in the secret police."

"You're not making me feel any safer here," Katie replied.

"Are you going to go to Bran the first thing in the morning or wait until after school?" Ruth asked.

"I'm not sure yet. I'll probably only know tomorrow."

FEELING VERY ALONE

Chapter 32

At breakfast, Katie was quiet. Her mind was very busy. "Ok," Katie finally said. "Why don't we wait until after school and go back to Bran? We'll look around again. Maybe we can find something. Maybe Anna will contact me, too," Katie said.

The others agreed.

After getting off their bus, Ruth, John, and Cam all walked into their classroom. Their classroom was the closest to the bus drop-off point. Katie's class was still farther away, so she started walking toward it.

As she was walking, she saw a taxi pull up in the street. Lupu didn't waste any time getting into the passenger side. Katie saw its driver was the one who overheard her the day before.

Oh, no. They're going to get there and find it first, she thought to herself. She felt she was letting Anna down. *Think, Katie, think! But, what can I do?* She instantly decided she needed to be at Bran castle as soon as possible, and she couldn't wait until after class. She ran down to the bus stop that was across the street from the college. They had stopped there on the bus ride back to Brașov the night before. She was hoping the bus going to Bran would stop there too.

She knew she'd be about 15 to 20 minutes behind Lupu, but she had to take that chance. She thought if she could at least be there if and when he found the gold, she could say or do something.

The bus was mercifully quick in getting to the stop and picking her up. She worried a bit since she hadn't had time to let her friends know what she was doing. She sent them a text while on the bus letting them know she was on her way to the castle.

The bus made good time, but for Katie, each minute dragged on as if it was an hour.

When the bus arrived at Bran, Katie jumped out and made her way up to the entrance of the castle. She bought her ticket and went inside. At first, she was relieved to be inside the castle. Then reality hit her. She still didn't know where to search for the gold. It's not that big of a castle unless you're looking for something and you don't know where it is, then it's huge. She also had another problem. She didn't want to run into Lupu or the taxi driver. The castle didn't feel as friendly as it was on her other visits. Alone, she saw a lot more shadows and they all looked like possible traps.

Katie needed to find Anna again. Anna would be Katie's best hope for finding the gold, and even though she was a ghost, Anna was the closest friend she had there.

A tour group must have unloaded a big bus after Katie got to the castle. There were lots of tourists all over. It made it more difficult for Katie to get around within the castle. Each time she tried to go into a room, or up some stairs, there were people in her way.

At one point, she saw Lupu and the taxi driver ahead of her. She just had enough time to duck behind some tourists and go into a side room before they could spot her. She could tell by the frustration on their faces that the tourists were slowing their search too.

The room Katie jumped into was an eating area of some type. She thought she might as well start her search in that room. On the walls were old photos of the grounds around the castle. When Katie looked at one of the photos, she felt that familiar cold draft come up from behind her. Before the room started to dull in color, Katie saw a familiar face in the photo. It was Anna. The photo was focused on Anna and another woman with two other people off in the background. The other woman was the other ghost. Before Katie could take a picture of the old photo, the cold came and she knew Anna would be coming. She didn't know if it was the cold, or the chance to talk to Anna, but she felt a boost of courage.

"*Dragă, ai venit din nou!*" Anna's voice said. But, before Katie had time to respond, the room started to spin again. Katie sensed two men standing in front of her. They were Lupu and the taxi driver. Up close they seemed very dangerous. With Anna gone and her friends not there, Katie felt very alone.

"You are looking for something?" Lupu asked. It sounded more like a statement to Katie. She wasn't sure what to say. She was sure they knew what she was looking for.

After a pause, Katie asked, "What do you mean? I'm here looking at Bran Castle."

"Now? When you should be in class," Lupu said. The two men stood close to Katie. They seemed experienced in intimidating people. "We know why you are here. You are looking for lost gold."

The taxi driver acted as a lookout, looking back and forth between Katie and the doorway. He must be watching for people who might come into the room.

"I don't know what you are talking about," Katie said.

"Oh, but you do," Lupu said. "You do know you are wasting your time, don't you? Anything you find here in Romania belongs to Romania. We still have laws that any 'national treasure' like gold, is the property of the Romanian government. It cannot be taken out of the country. If you know where it is, you'd better tell me."

With that, he grabbed Katie's arm and started walking her out the door and down the stairs. She tried to squirm out of his grip, but his hand held her like an iron trap. She knew she didn't have any other option but to go with him. Katie wasn't sure what he intended to do with her. She was glad there were other people in the castle. "Let go of me," Katie said over and over again. Confused tourists stepped to the side to let them pass, as Lupu said, "*Stai acolo! Poliție, Police!*" Katie was pretty sure Lupu wasn't a police officer anymore, but she didn't know what she could say about it. The taxi driver followed them down to the main door of the castle.

Katie was happy when Lupu finally let go of her arm. With a slight shove, he said "Go back to school, now!" The taxi driver stepped next to Lupu and they both stood in front of the castle entrance with their arms crossed. Katie knew her only option at that point was to leave. She was mad, and the ache in her arm where Lupu held it didn't help her feel any better. She wanted to do something but didn't know what. Being a foreigner, and only speaking a little of the language, Katie knew she could not stand up to Lupu by herself.

Katie made her way down the path from the castle to the base of the hill. From there, she looked back to make sure Lupu or the driver had not followed her. She could tell they thought they frightened her away. *They don't know who they're dealing with*, Katie thought. She was set on getting back into the castle and finding the gold first. Katie made her way toward the Chapel outside the castle where she had seen Anna before.

Katie checked her phone to see where her friends were. The app on her phone showed they were still at the school. She texted them to be careful of Lupu and the taxi driver. Katie explained what had happened and told them not to come yet. She had been working on a plan and needed to check on a few things first. She then turned her phone to silent.

Katie tried to stay off the path as much as possible on her way to the chapel. She didn't want to take the chance of Lupu looking out a window and seeing her.

Approaching the chapel, she saw the doors open. The familiar young woman knelt there in prayer.

"Anna, I need your help," she said. Before Katie could say anything more, the young woman was standing in front of her.

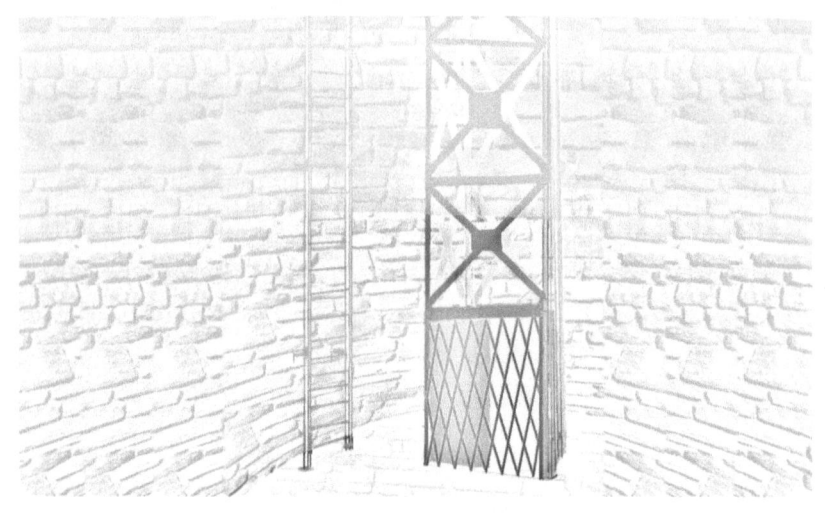

NOW, TO GET BACK INSIDE

Chapter 33

" **T**wo men. They will not let me take your gift. They made me leave the castle," Katie told Anna. She hoped her Romanian was good enough for Anna to understand.

Anna nodded and held her hand out to Katie. Katie took a deep breath in and put her hand in Anna's. She half expected her hand to go straight through Anna's, but it didn't. Although Anna's hand was ice cold, it still felt firm. Katie felt comforted.

Anna started to lead her farther down the path. Ahead on the trail, Katie spied an old metal door on the side of the hill. When they got to the door, Katie found it was already open. She hesitated to step inside but knew she didn't have many options. *You can do this*, she told herself and stepped into the dark tunnel.

Anna firmly held Katie's hand as Anna led her through the winding tunnels. There was a slight glow from Anna, but it wasn't enough to light up the tunnels. Katie was amazed they were not bumping into any walls or low walkways. It was as if there was some sort of protective bubble keeping them from hitting the rock walls. Even still, Katie worried that there might be bats in the low, dark tunnels, and she didn't want to run into them. She was glad she was wearing sturdy shoes so she didn't have to worry so much about what she was walking in.

They walked for about five minutes before they came across an old, rusty looking metal cage. Tall metal bars were all around the cage. The bars rose up into the darkness. Across the front of the cage were some criss crossed bars that reminded Katie of a pet fence, yet taller.

As she looked more closely at the cage, she figured out it was an old elevator. *Those metal rails must be some sort of track the elevator used to go up and down on*, she thought. From what she could see, none of it looked safe. The cables were rusty and had cobwebs on a large pulley wheel above the cage.

Katie had trouble seeing the cage clearly. She took out her phone and used its light to see better. Katie couldn't help but cry out when she saw a few rats scurry out of the old elevator. After she was sure that the rats left, she peeked into the elevator.

The cage looked firmly rusted in place. She didn't want to try it even if it worked, she wouldn't know how. There were no buttons in it, only a large lever and some knobs.

Her light came upon an old rusty ladder attached to the elevator shaft wall. Even though the ladder looked scarier to Katie than the elevator, she knew it would be the better choice. Anna had brought her there to get back up into the castle. So, she tucked her phone in the pocket of her shirt with the light still shining out. She was extra happy she chose that particular shirt to wear that day.

Rust had eaten away at much of the metal ladder. Katie found it harder to grip the rungs of the ladder than she expected. The rust was sharp in places and hurt her hands. *Am I going to have any skin on my hands by the time I get to the top of this?* she asked herself. The rust on the rungs wasn't the only thing about the ladder that worried Katie. The drips of water from above and the water on the sides of the shaft made her confidence fade even more. She hoped the bolts holding the ladder to the rock walls were not too rusted.

Katie went up the ladder, only one rung at a time. She made sure her running shoes had a good grip on each one. Anna encouraged Katie the entire way up the shaft. Anna, with her glow, drifted up the shaft like a balloon.

Katie made sure to not look down. Even a simple glance was enough to make her knees go a little weak. Halfway up the ladder, pain started shooting through her forearms from gripping the rungs so tightly. At last, she came up to a level with a small platform. It was the top of the trip for the elevator. There had been no other platforms the entire way up.

Moving that first leg away from the ladder, across the open empty space to the platform, took all of Katie's courage and willpower. *Ok, this is the scariest place I've ever been in,* Katie thought to herself. *I only wanted to come to summer school and learn the language. Now, I'm hanging on a rusty old ladder, probably 100-feet in the air, following a ghost, to get some gold that some bad guys want. The only thing that would make this worse is if my mom ever finds out about this.*

She brought her thoughts back to getting the rest of her body off the ladder.

She worked up her courage and pushed herself off the ladder and got her other leg onto the platform. *Whew, I made it! What's next?* she thought. She flattened herself against the wall, and it gave her a small sense of security.

The dampness and strain of climbing the long ladder were draining Katie's strength. She hoped it wasn't affecting her thinking. She needed to be clear-headed for whatever would be coming up next. After taking a couple of deep breaths, she steadied herself.

Katie hadn't thought about how long her climb took until she pulled the phone out of her pocket to use its light. The phone showed it was 5:40 p.m. *The castle will close in 20 minutes. The crowd of tourists is probably gone by now. Lupu and the driver should be gone when the castle closes, too. I'll wait here until closing time at 6 o'clock. Then, I'll just have to avoid the security guys. They could all be like Lupu. How many did I see before? I wish I could remember.*

While waiting 20 minutes, Katie tried to use her phone to text her friends to let them know what she was doing and where she was. It didn't work. *These thick walls must be blocking the service here. I'm in a dead zone,* she thought and gave her weak joke a weak laugh. The whole time climbing the ladder she felt Anna's cold presence. She looked up from her phone and saw Anna in the shaft watching her. *Who am I kidding? I am DEFINITELY in a dead zone!*

Katie typed out a text to Cam, in case she came across a place that had service. Sometimes, her text messages would still be sent even with a poor connection. *It's worth a try*, she thought.

Next, Katie turned off the light on her phone. *Don't waste your battery*, she thought. It turned out that waiting in the dark was harder to do than she first thought it would be. Every new noise caused her to tense. She was sure she was hearing the sounds of rats coming closer. Katie had to make herself relax by repeating to herself, over and over again, *I've got this*.

FINDING A WAY IN

Chapter 34

After enough time passed, Katie directed her light around the platform and found a steel rod coming out of the wall at the side of what looked like an old wooden door. She studied the door as best she could, but there was no latch or knob. She then turned her attention to the iron bar. It had a small plate at the end of it. The bar looked like it went into a hole in the stone that was a little bigger than the thickness of the bar. Katie tried to turn it like a doorknob, but it wouldn't turn. Then, she gave it a push, and it still wasn't moving.

"Great, now what?" she asked herself out loud.

Anna said something in Romanian, but Katie didn't understand. When Anna saw Katie didn't understand, she made a motion with her hands. She pushed with both hands as if there was something for her to push.

Katie nodded and used both of her hands to give the bar a second try. This time, she pushed harder. The wooden door opened only a fraction of an inch, but it did move. Katie gave the door another push on the left side of the door. It started to swing open. She stepped through the doorway and right away felt relieved to be out of the scary shaft. She was happy to be on firm flooring and inside the warmer castle.

She looked around and saw she was in the castle's great hall. Walking a few feet into the room, she turned to examine the doorway she had just come through. The door turned out to be a section of paneling on a wall that looked like all the other paneling in the room. It looked like it was never meant to move.

At first, Katie was going to just close the door, and then she had a second thought. *I'd better look for some kind of latch in the door to see if I can open it from this side*, she thought. Anna must have thought the same thing because she moved to the door and pointed to a small metal lever on the side of the panel. It was the exact color of the wood and difficult to see, even with her light. Katie lifted the lever and saw the locking mechanism move. "Got it!" she said, shutting the panel and making sure it would work later. Katie closed it again so no one would find it.

Once more, Anna led Katie through the hall to a short staircase. They went up the few stairs and stopped by an opening in the wall. Katie recognized where she was now. They were at the bottom of a secret stairway. Well, at one time it was a secret. Now it was part of the route for tourists to take. The steps were steep and the walls were narrow. The walls and the arched roof were all made out of large stones. There was a rope handle to help people as they walked up the stairs. Katie remembered going up these stairs with Cam a couple of days before.

Katie stopped to listen to a creaking sound. It sounded like people were walking upstairs. She quickly climbed the stairs to catch up with Anna. Anna got almost up to the top of the three-story staircase and stopped. She pointed to a stone just above her head on the wall. It had a symbol carved into it. The symbol was a simple crown above the letter M.

Right away, Katie saw it was the same symbol on the back of her necklace. Then, strangely, Katie saw Anna point to another stone much lower on the opposite wall. Anna then stretched out her hand and foot. Katie understood. "Are you telling me to use both my hand and foot to push the stones in? Do they need to be pushed at the same time?"

She went up to where she could push the stones. First, she tried to push each one-at-a-time, in case that would work. Neither stone moved. They felt so strongly stuck in place that Katie worried if she would have enough strength to move them at all.

Katie reached out placing her fingertips on the upper stone. Then, she pointed her opposite foot at the lower stone. She was barely able to reach them, and just an inch or two short of being able to push them both at the same time. She stopped to think. *There must be a way to get an inch or two closer.* It came to her quickly. She took off one of her shoes and used it to push the higher stone while she used her foot on the lower stone. It worked. She was able to reach both stones and push on them at the same time.

The stones moved more easily than she thought they would. Apparently, both stones needed to be moved at the same time to get either one to move at all.

Katie listened after pushing on the stones. She expected some part of the wall or staircase to make noise opening up or see something move. Nothing happened. She turned to Anna in hopes of getting another direction.

From the top of the stairs, Anna was nodding at Katie and motioning that she should come up the rest of the way. Katie wasn't sure if that was the response she was hoping for. *Why did I have to push in the stones first?* she thought.

Katie poked her head slowly out of the stairway before entering the room. She had remembered hearing people walking around on the floor above her earlier. She hoped they wouldn't still be there. No one was there and then the reason came to her. The stairs she came up traveled up two stories, not only one. Now, those people would be on the floor below the one she was now on. She knew she'd have to walk softly so she took off her other shoe and carried them both.

Katie saw that she and Anna were in the music room. It was a large space with a high ceiling supported by dark wooden beams. It also had large wooden bookcases filled with books. Inside the room was a smaller sitting area built out from a wall. This area had two short walls and a low roof over the area to give the feeling of a cozy reading space. It was like a room within a room. A fireplace sat in the sitting room's wall, across from a padded bench. Anna stood by the fireplace and pointed to it. Katie used her phone's flashlight to light up the area better. She could see a metal pan under the logs in the fireplace. The pan looked like it was not set in all the way on the right side. Anna kept pointing to the right side of that pan.

Good thing there's no fire in there right now, Katie thought to herself as she took hold of the pan and pulled. She found she was able to swing the firebox pan out, logs and all. It was easier to move than she thought it would be.

She shined her flashlight into the opening left by the logs and immediately had to close her eyes. The sudden golden glare was like someone taking a picture with the flash on. She moved her light to the side. There were three wood chests sitting there. The two large chests were open and filled with what looked like gold coins.

There was a smaller box sitting there with its lid closed. A yellowed, dusty folded piece of paper sat on top of that box. The paper had a wax seal on it. Katie picked up the paper and blew off the dust. Katie wasn't ready for what she was about to see. Written on the paper in fancy letters, was *Anna Cristea*. Katie's heart thumped loudly in her chest. She turned to Anna. Again, Anna was nodding to her. Anna had a broad smile on her face and her arms folded across her chest.

Katie broke the seal and opened the letter, holding it out for Anna to see. The Romanian was difficult for Katie to read. She could make out one part that said in Romanian, '*for Anna Cristea*' and another part, '*this _____ of gold.*' "Wow," Katie whispered. "Anna, this is for you. And it's signed by Her Majesty, Queen Marie!"

Katie was aware there might still be others in the castle and she had to be as quiet as possible. Her excitement made being quiet all the more difficult. She wanted to shout for joy. She was so excited to find proof that her relative had a connection to the queen of Romania, as well as a treasure. *Wait until I tell Mom and Dad,* she thought.

TEARS OF A GHOST

Chapter 35

Katie was amazed. After a long moment, Katie opened the small box. Inside were coins of gold like in the other two chests. Katie took one of the coins in her hand, flipping it over to see both sides. She had never seen a coin like it before. It had a bird holding a crown on one side. The other side had three people, maybe soldiers.

She put the coin back in the box and held it out to Anna. It looked to Katie like Anna was crying. Tears were running down her face.

Katie could hear the word *nepoata* echoing until the echoes were too faint to hear anymore. Pride grew inside Katie. She knew *nepoata* meant 'granddaughter' in Romanian.

In the distance, footsteps replaced Anna's voice. Katie held the box and letter in one hand and swung the firebox closed. It latched in place with a loud click.

Looking back to see if anyone was coming, Katie's heart sank when she saw Lupu standing there inside the doorway. *He must have seen the hiding place*, she thought. Katie dashed over to the stairway followed by Anna. As they rushed past the stones in the stairway wall, Katie noticed the stones were back into place. *At least he couldn't have seen how to open it*, Katie realized.

Katie was surprised Lupu hadn't already started down the stairs until she looked back over her shoulder. Anna was back at the top of the stairs. *I'll bet Anna's giving Lupu the scare he deserves*, she thought.

Back on the first floor, Katie managed to hold Anna's box and letter under one arm. She had to slip her shoes back onto her feet. She couldn't carry her shoes, the box, and the letter for much longer. Also, she knew she needed shoes on her feet to make it down that ladder. Katie hated to do it, but after she got her shoes on, she took the folded letter and stuck it in her back pocket. She picked up the box and headed to the wall panel. Lupu and his friend were coming down the stairs. The men exchanged heated words as they each tried to enter the narrow stairway at the same time. Anna had only been able to slow the men with what she had done to scare them. They were still coming.

Katie slipped the lever up and popped open the panel. She jumped inside and almost slammed it closed behind her. The letter fell out of her pocket as she jumped. She was too focused on getting away from the two men to see it float down the elevator shaft. It settled down to the ground on the far side of the old elevator's cage.

How was it that Lupu and the driver were still there after closing time? Pushing aside that train of thought, Katie stepped out onto the platform in the elevator shaft. Katie shined her phone light on the ladder. She put the phone back in her top pocket with the light on to make it easier to see. She knew she had to take the time to do that. Otherwise, she wouldn't be able to see where she needed to go.

Time was short. She wasn't sure if Lupu already knew of or could find the secret panel. She leaned out toward the ladder with one hand and realized it was going to be even harder going down the ladder. This time she had to carry the heavy box in one hand. That only left her one hand to hold on to the ladder. She forced herself to go down as fast as she could even though her hand hurt from the rust. She looked down once but right away made up her mind to never do that again. Her knees started to go weak and the only thing she could think about was trying not to fall. She became frozen for a moment, too scared to move. It was the pounding she heard that made her move again. Lupu must have been trying to get the door open. She returned her attention to getting down the ladder that seemed to disappear into an endless space of black nothingness below her.

She forced herself to keep going to the floor of the elevator shaft. Anna directed her through the maze of tunnels. This time, Katie tried to make mental notes of where she was going. She left her flashlight on and Anna still had a glow around her which allowed Katie to see the path. Katie was sure she could find her way back in the future if needed.

Stopping at the tunnel's opening to catch her breath, Katie realized Anna was no longer with her. She could tell because she was missing the chill that was always around when Anna was present. *I wish you'd stay a little longer*, she thought.

As Katie stepped into the cool night air, she was surprised to find her friends standing there. "How'd you guys get here?" she asked.

"By taxi," Ruth said.

"We haven't been here long. We got to the base of the mountain and saw on my phone that you were over here somewhere," Cam added. "So, we followed the path and found you coming out of that old door."

"Yeah, creepy old door," John added.

"We found a box of gold and a letter," Katie said.

"We?" asked Cam.

"Yeah. Anna was with me."

"So, you've got gold coins in that box?" John asked.

"Sure do. They're for Anna!" Katie said.

"They're for a ghost?" asked Ruth.

"Yes. The letter here in my pocket was with the box. Queen Marie left Anna the letter back in the 1930s. It seems no one knew about this gold or the other chests of gold."

"Yes, the chests of gold," said a deeper man's voice in the darkness. It was Lupu's voice. "You cannot keep any of that gold," he said. "It all belongs to Romania. Give that to me now and tell me how to open that chamber."

None of the teens believed Lupu wanted to give the gold to the government. They were pretty sure he wanted to keep it for himself. Probably some for anyone who helped him, like the taxi driver, Radu, and that guy who grabbed Katie's necklace. But, the majority of it would be for him.

Lupu and the driver stepped out of the darkness, panting and red-faced. They came toward Katie. The other teens stepped in front of Katie and the box.

There was a determined look on Lupu's and the driver's faces. They pushed the teens apart. Lupu got close enough to grab Katie's arm. It made her drop the box and it opened when it hit the ground. Some of the gold coins spilled out onto the gravel pathway.

It took Lupu only a split second to mutter, "*Aurul dacic!*" Dacian gold! His eyes grew wide.

Ruth was the first to hear it. Then, everyone heard the thumping sounds. The cab driver took half a step back and looked at Lupu, not knowing if he would say something.

Everyone felt the cold draft that dropped on them like a giant bucket of ice water. Everyone, except Katie, saw the figure of a woman appear behind her. The figure was faint at first. Ruth grabbed John's arm for support. Cam stopped on his way to Katie. The thumps grew louder as the woman grew more visible.

The woman was clear now. On her head sat a gold crown. She held up her open hand, saying in Romanian, "*Stop! Stop! Stop!*" Her command to 'Stop!' echoed through the cold night air.

Lupu and the driver grew up in Romania after the days of Kings and Queens. They grew up in communist times. They would never listen to this woman, even if she had been a queen. They did not think of her as a threat. They were wrong.

THE QUEEN STEPS IN
Chapter 36

I n an instant, Lupu and the driver saw no one around them except the Queen. For them, her appearance changed just as fast. First, they saw only this woman. The next second a skeleton stood in front of them. Its heart was pulsing within its bony chest. The loud thumping sound came from the skeleton's beating heart. It pointed an outstretched hand at them. "*Faceți nimic! Faceți nimic!* (Do nothing!)" it commanded. The two men screamed in terror. Fear overcame them. They wanted to run, but they lost control over their legs. They were stuck as if nails held their shoes to the ground. All they could do was close their eyes.

The three teens heard the thumping sounds but could only see the ghostly Queen with her crown and scepter, not a skeleton.

They also saw Anna standing behind Katie. Their vision was of the queen with her hand on Anna's shoulder. Anna had her hand over Katie's shoulder. Katie felt the cold from Anna's hand, but didn't know why Lupu and the driver were so terrified. She thought it best not to turn around. She didn't want to know what the ghosts were doing.

"Katie!" Ruth said. That's Queen Marie with Anna! That's Her Majesty, Marie." And with that, Ruth gave a short bow.

Katie turned and saw the queen. The queen gave her a loving smile and a short nod.

Katie froze there, not knowing what to do or say next.

The queen spoke to Katie in short, echoing words. "*Leave. Leave. Leave.* Katie knew that was an order.

"We have to leave, NOW!" Katie said to her friends.

Cam said, "We still have the taxi we came in. We told him to wait. It's time to get out of here!"

"Yes, you're quite right," said Ruth.

"Definitely," said Katie. And with that, she turned to Anna. "I will make sure this gets to your granddaughter." She then turned to the queen, "Your majesty. Thank you." Then, Katie curtsied before the queen. She thought that might be the best thing to do since she'd seen it done in movies all the time.

Katie picked up the box and the others helped by grabbing the coins that had spilled out earlier. They put most of them in the box and a few in Katie's hand.

"Come on," Cam told them, trying to hurry Katie. Katie put the last of the coins in the box and closed it. They hurried for the taxi, leaving Lupu and his friend behind. They ran, not knowing how much time they would have before Lupu and the driver showed up at their taxi.

Relief flooded over the teens as they saw their taxi was waiting for them. They got inside and were on their way back to their dorm.

"Do you think this gold will be safe overnight in your dorm room?" Cam asked the others.

"Oh, yes. I'd say so," Katie replied. "Lupu and his friend are frozen with fear. He won't be coming after us. And, I have Anna who has been watching over me pretty well."

"I'm sure glad she's on our side," Cam said.

LUPU, THE DRIVER, AND THE QUEEN

Chapter 37

L upu and the driver couldn't see Katie and the others leave the castle grounds. Anna and the Queen's presence froze the two men in place. They were only aware of Anna, the Queen, and the beating heart.

After knowing Katie was safe, the two ghosts vanished. Even though they were gone, Lupu and his friend found they couldn't move. The two realized they were 'unfrozen' when they collapsed onto the gravel path they stood upon. As soon as they could get to their feet, the two ran away at full speed. The men screamed like frightened little children.

Even running the entire way back to their taxi, Lupu and his friend got there after everyone had left. The two men stood there only long enough to unlock the taxi and get inside. The driver started the car immediately, and the tires made a screeching sound as they hastily drove away. "What was that?" the taxi driver asked Lupu over and over again. He had a hard time holding the steering wheel, his hands were shaking so much.

"I have no idea," Lupu managed to get out. "But I did see that gold."

"I'm not touching that gold," the driver said. "I'm no fool. Do you want to be a dead man?" he asked Lupu.

"You are a fool. No, you don't have to touch that gold. You will get nothing! No 'spirit' will stop me." He said the word, spirit, with a great deal of contempt. There was still some fear in Lupu, but he kept it to himself. "And, if you tell anyone about it, you will be a dead man! You know I do what I say."

WHAT TO DO WITH THIS GOLD NOW?

Chapter 38

Cam and John met Katie and Ruth in the girls' dorm room. They were careful to be quiet. They didn't want to get into trouble. Boys weren't supposed to be in a girl's dorm room with the door shut, but this was important. Of course, the teens weren't going to talk about the gold with their door open.

"We need to find someone who can help us," Katie said. "This is huge."

"I agree. I wish we knew more people here that we could trust." Cam said.

"Let's talk to our teacher," Ruth suggested. "She said her husband works in the government."

"Yeah, you're right. She did say something about him." John added. "Let's talk to her tomorrow before class."

"I guess that's the best we can do for now," Cam said. He wasn't sure she was the best person to talk to about so much money, but he didn't have any better answers.

"Are you sure?" Katie asked. After all, she had never met their teacher. She thought of her teacher but she didn't know anything about him. After their run-ins with Lupu, she wasn't comfortable trusting a man she didn't know well.

"Should we divide up the money, so you don't have to be responsible for all of it, Katie?" Cam asked. "I don't want Lupu or anyone grabbing you for the gold."

"Thanks," Katie said. "I'll be fine with it. I've got my backpack to keep it in, and I've got Anna to watch over me, too. She and the Queen are going to be our best defense. Besides, they might think you're trying to take some of it and go after you."

"You're spot on, there," Ruth added. "All the same, I'm going to prop a chair up against our door tonight."

"Well, sounds like a plan then. John and I will meet you here in the morning. We can go downstairs together. Why don't we skip the cafeteria and get something to eat on the way to school? It'd be better to avoid Lupu that way," Cam said.

"That sounds great. I don't know what I'd do without you guys," Katie said. John stepped toward the door to open it. Before he or Cam could leave, Katie held John's arm and gave him a slight kiss on the cheek. "Thank you." She then took Cam's arm and gave him a longer kiss on his cheek.

"Thank you!" Cam said with a smile on his face, touching the spot where she kissed him.

Katie closed the door, locked it, and leaned with her back against it. She stared off, lost in thought. Ruth said, "Let's prop that door to stay shut." Katie's attention jumped back to the task at hand. The two girls slid a chair from the desk in the room to the door. Katie pushed the back of the chair up under the doorknob. She wiggled the chair and after being satisfied it was secure, returned to her bed.

"It's been quite a day," Katie said.

"My thoughts exactly," Ruth said.

Katie emptied her backpack. Then, she put the small chest of gold inside. When she reached into her back pocket for the letter, she gasped. "It's not there. The letter!" she said. There was a slight panic in her voice. "I've got to have that letter!"

Ruth said, "You've got the gold. That's what counts."

"You don't understand. Without the letter, I'll never have a chance of keeping this. There's no way to prove it was a gift from the queen to my great-great-grandma. We're going to have to find that letter. Well, I'm going to have to find it." The girls looked over the entire room but didn't find it anywhere. Katie and Ruth even went down the stairs and all the way to where they got out of the taxi. "It might have fallen out of my pocket when I went through that passageway. Or, maybe even in that elevator shaft. I don't know. So much was happening."

"Sounds like we'll be returning to Bran tomorrow. We'll check there," Ruth said.

GETTING HELP, NOT SLEEP

Chapter 39

No one slept well that night.

"I kept tossing and turning," Cam told John, "all night."

"I know what you mean. I did too." John said. "I'll bet Lupu and that other guy got even less sleep."

"I sure hope so," Cam said. "What a creep and a thief. I've always said that guy was slimy. You know he won't be turning any of that found gold into the government."

"If he did, I'd bet it'd only be a fraction of what's there. I'm sure he wants all the chests of gold!"

"Do you think we'll get any kind of reward?" John asked.

"Maybe. If the government didn't give any kind of reward for people turning in lost Dacian gold, nobody would probably turn any in. I'm glad Katie's family will be getting something."

"Good point."

After John and Cam got ready, they knocked on the girls' door. "It's us," John said.

After unlocking it, Katie opened the door enough to peek out. When she was sure it was only Cam and John, she opened it. The girls were ready and had been waiting for the boys. They walked out; Katie had her backpack on. She normally didn't bring her backpack. This time she had to. The box was too big and heavy for her smaller shoulder bag. Cam could tell there was something wrong from the look on Katie's face.

"What's wrong?" he asked.

Katie reluctantly told Cam about having lost the letter. She felt so embarrassed because it was so important.

"Don't worry, we'll find it," Cam assured her.

Outside, they felt a little safer in the morning sunlight. They walked to the school, stopping at a coffee shop along the way to pick up breakfast. They ate while they walked.

Once at the college, they went right to Cam, John, and Ruth's classroom. The teacher hadn't gotten there yet. They decided they'd check out their teacher's office, in case she was there. It was close by, and they thought privacy would be better there, anyway.

They climbed the old stone stairs in the building that held the professors' offices. They were relieved to find Mrs. Popescu in her office. She was eating her breakfast while going over her lesson plans for the day.

"*Bună studenți*. You are here early today. Can I help you with something?" she said with a friendly smile on her face.

"Mrs. Popescu. You said your husband works in the government, didn't you?" Cam asked.

"Yes. He is an *Inspector de poliție*. That means he is a police inspector. Why do you ask?"

"We found something and it's very important," Katie said. "Although you may not believe us," Katie warned. "Here goes," she said. She then told Mrs. Popescu the entire story about finding the gold for her great-great-grandmother. She told her about Lupu and his friend. She did hesitate to tell her about the ghosts though. She knew it would be difficult for this woman to believe ghosts helped her.

Mrs. Popescu's face said a lot. She didn't believe their story. "Are you sure?" she asked.

"Show Mrs. P the letter," John suggested.

Katie looked embarrassed. "That's the thing. I can't find the letter. It must have fallen out of my pocket when I was being chased in the castle."

Mrs. Popescu's face started to show even more doubt until Katie pulled out the small chest of gold coins. Seeing it, Mrs. Popescu had to sit back in her chair.

"Do you know what you have here?" she asked. "Why, this is incredible! If this is indeed Dacian gold, this might be worth a small fortune."

"Will the government let me keep it?" Katie asked. "I know they don't let things this old out of the country. Remember, it was a gift from Queen Marie."

"Well, it seems this was a gift to your family, if you can find the letter and it is authentic," she said. "Of course, it would have to be found and verified first. We have a professor who is an expert on this. Oh, what did you say your relative's name was, Anna Cristea? And, you said she lived in Bran, near the castle?" Mrs. Popescu wrote the information down on a piece of paper before picking up the phone. "I'll call my husband right now."

About 25 minutes later, Police Inspector Popescu arrived. He was interested in the story the teens had to tell about the gold and Lupu.

Mrs. Popescu believed the teens when they said Lupu tried to steal the gold. "I'll bet he will be trying to get the other chests, too," Katie told them.

"I'm sure you're right," the Inspector said. "We have been investigating him for some time. We suspect he did a lot of illegal things when he was in the *Securitate*. We didn't have proof. If we can catch him keeping the gold, we will have him. But, to arrest him, we will need to see that he has the gold and does not plan to return it."

Katie said, "I have an idea how we could catch him." She told everyone her plan.

"It sounds like it might work. We'll try it," the Inspector said, but his next words upset Katie.

"We will have to hold on to this gold for now," he told her.

Katie's heart sank. All the teens felt let down. They knew the government still did some bad things. Katie worried, *Are these the people my mother told me to be careful about? Is there still a lot of corruption in Romania?* They had been hopeful they'd be able to keep some of the gold. Now it looked like they might not get any of it.

"I know what you are thinking," the Inspector said. "It's written across your faces. Do not worry. We are not keeping it. At least, I'm not. I'll do my best to get what is rightfully yours."

Katie felt a little better, though not fully reassured.

LAYING A TRAP
Chapter 40

"Remember, this will not be easy," the Inspector said. "We need to hear him say he is going to keep the gold or see him hide it in some way. He may be difficult to capture. He is former *Securitate*. They were and are still dangerous men. Lupu knows if he is caught with the gold, he can say he didn't have time to turn it over to the authorities."

After they left the inspector, Katie and her friends couldn't get his words of caution out of their heads. They decided to not go to their classes that day. They didn't want to run into Lupu. Shortly before lunch, Katie and her friends took the bus to Bran. Since they didn't have the chest on them to worry about, they thought it would be best to use their time to search for the letter.

Lupu also kept away from the students until he had a solid plan of what to do next. He knew he needed to go back for the gold before Katie removed it from the castle. He calculated that he had some time because Katie and her friends were young and probably didn't know what to do next. They couldn't just go into the castle during the day and retrieve two chests of gold. The castle's security would find them right away. *Even they would know that*, he thought.

Lupu did not lack confidence. He scared lots of people during his days in the *Securitate*. He planned to do the same to these kids if he needed to, even if they had some kind of spirit to help them.

Inspector Popescu had arranged for one of his men to keep an eye on Lupu the whole day. They thought it best to know where he was so they could be ready for him. The police were convinced Lupu would not try to take the gold from the castle during the day. It would be too difficult to hide. They thought he would go back at night.

The police watched Lupu get into a car and drive off late in the afternoon. They tried to keep up with him, but they lost him. After he found out Lupu was no longer in sight, the Inspector told his men at the castle to be ready just in case.

However, Lupu had already returned to the castle. He was inside at that moment. Earlier, he called in some favors from former *Securitate* members. Those former *Securitate* knew the castle from top to bottom. They told him about the secret entrance and the elevator. He had never heard of the elevator there before. He was surprised the girl knew about it, but that night he would put it to better use. With Radu, Lupu snuck in the same way Katie must have the previous night. They made their way up the elevator shaft to wait. Lupu wanted to go into the castle just before closing time. He knew the guards would be changing then and there might be some tourists leaving. They could blend in if needed. While at the top of the shaft, Lupu found the lever to open the secret panel.

Katie and her friends rode the bus to Bran Castle. They retraced their steps outside the castle from the taxi stand, back to where Lupu found Katie and the ghosts. Nothing! The next place to look was inside the castle. Katie felt it was safe enough since it was still daylight and the castle was open to the public. They were sure Lupu wouldn't show up at the castle during the day.

John smelled *clătite* cooking as they walked to the path leading to the castle. He had to stop. He was still hungry, even though he had eaten lunch before they left. "I'm going to grab a *clătite* super quick. You guys can go on and I'll catch up," John said.

Katie saw that Cam also stopped. She said, "Cam, go ahead and get one too if you want. It's bright daylight and I'm sure Lupu won't be here yet."

Cam hesitated, briefly. "We won't be long." He walked over to where John was already placing his order.

The girls looked at each other. "How can they eat at a time like this?" Katie asked. Ruth could only shrug. The two girls kept walking, but Katie stopped off the pathway to the castle to tie her shoe.

Ruth, being anxious to help her friend find the letter, kept walking. She knew it would only be a minute or two before Katie caught up with her.

Ruth didn't notice the three men coming down from the castle. They walked past Ruth. She was behind some other tourists on the path. But, they did see her three friends further behind.

The men stopped the students and pulled out their badges. "You must not go up to the castle now," one of the policemen said. "We have swept the grounds, and Lupu is not there yet."

The men took the students to a nearby building, told them to wait inside, and assigned an officer to watch them. The orders didn't seem fair to Katie or the boys, but they knew they were in a foreign country and laws were different here. They didn't want to get into trouble.

Ruth reached the top of the hill and looked back for Katie. Katie wasn't on the path. Then, she started looking farther back for John and Cam. *I guess Katie wanted to walk with Cam. She's probably waiting for them to finish their food. They should be here straight away*, she thought.

LET ME SHOW YOU AROUND
Chapter 41

Ruth bought her ticket and went inside the castle. She was going to start looking for the letter until she saw the well in the courtyard. She was curious about it after what Katie had told her. She went to look down inside of it. Through the grate on top of the opening, she could make out machinery. *That must have been where the elevator shaft came from*, she thought to herself. She marveled at the thought of Katie climbing such a tall ladder, especially in the dark. *I'm glad I'll never have to do something like that*, she thought.

While she was out in the courtyard by the well, Radu was upstairs looking out from a window. He saw Ruth and immediately went to tell Lupu. Lupu stayed out of sight because he worried the castle guards might be looking for him. He thought no one would be looking for Radu. So he decided to use Radu as a lookout and as extra muscle when it came time to carry the heavy gold.

"Do you see any of her friends with her?" Lupu asked.

"No, not yet," Radu said. They knew if Ruth was there, the others weren't too far behind.

Lupu told Radu to go down and get Ruth to the top of the castle. He had a plan to make Katie help him. Radu went without waiting for an explanation. Lupu wasn't surprised Radu didn't ask any questions. *Radu is stupid.* Of course, Lupu felt everyone was stupid compared to himself. *Radu would be a good one to leave for the police to catch after I get the gold,* he thought.

Radu found Ruth outside the torture museum. She had come in from the courtyard and was heading through the hallway. Radu was not a welcome sight. She knew he was friends with Lupu. She started to worry. She hoped John and the others would get there soon.

"Hello," Radu said. "I thought you visited here already."

"Ah, yes," Ruth said. "It's so interesting here. What are you doing here?" she asked.

"Oh, me? I like to come here. I volunteer here sometimes," he lied. "Let me show you around. Answer any questions you might have. Here, let's start in here." He held out his arm to direct Ruth into the Torture Museum. Ruth was uneasy and didn't want to go in there with Radu.

"I've been in there already. I was going to start at the top floor and work my way down," she said. She wanted to get to the upper levels where Katie might have dropped that letter, but she knew she couldn't tell Radu about the letter.

Radu agreed, even though he wasn't so happy with that. He wanted to wait before bringing her to Lupu. He thought it would be better if he got her there closer to closing time. There would be fewer people around. "Are you sure?" he asked. "There are some interesting things in here," he said.

"I'm sure there are. You certainly may go inside, if you like. Don't let me stop you."

Radu knew he wasn't going to be able to stall her much, so he decided to go with her upstairs now. The way Radu acted worried Ruth. He was too pushy. She thought about not going with him, but she was also afraid he would be suspicious about her being at the castle. She went with him thinking there would probably be a lot of people inside the castle. Hopefully, guards walking around, too.

The two didn't say much as they climbed the winding wooden stairs up to the top level of the castle. Radu read out loud the posted signs they came across. He wanted her to think he knew more about the castle than he did.

Ruth was feeling more and more that Radu was a threat when she hadn't seen others after a while. She kept hoping her friends would show up. She couldn't guess what was holding them up for so long. Still a little fearful, she looked around as much as she could for that letter while they walked.

The two finally reached the top floor. There, they walked through a study and a game room. Ruth scanned the floor for the letter. She was standing at the doorway between the game room and a small bedroom when she felt someone put their hand over her mouth and an arm around her waist. She tried to break loose, but the strong arms pulled her back. She grabbed the doorway, but couldn't hold on to it. She looked to Radu for some help. He didn't move or show any signs of surprise. It didn't take her long to figure out who was holding her. *I knew I shouldn't have trusted Radu*, she thought. Her attacker pulled her into what looked like a closet. Ruth tried to kick and make noise, but she was no match for Lupu.

Lupu slammed the door shut, keeping both of them inside the closet. Ruth was becoming frantic. She struggled until she saw the flash of a knife blade waving in front of her eyes. Her whole body stiffened in fright, just before everything went black.

DETAINED

Chapter 42

Katie knew it was getting late. It was closing time for the castle and they still hadn't heard anything from Ruth. Katie was starting to worry. John was pacing the room. Katie knew he was worried, too.

Katie had come up with a plan. She walked to the policeman and said, "We would like to go back to Braşov now." The policeman didn't understand her English so she said it simply, in her best Romanian. "*Noi dorim sa mergem apoi la Braşov.*"

Now he understood what she was saying. He motioned for them to stay there. He didn't say anything. He just looked upset. *I hope he can't make that decision*, Katie thought. She was right. He would need to go ask his boss. Again, he motioned to the teens and said, "*Stați!*" Then, he left the room and locked the door behind him.

"We've gotta get out of here and see what's happened to Ruth," Katie whispered to the two boys. John nodded in agreement. Cam looked out the window.

"I don't see anybody," he said. "Maybe we can sneak out." He tried the door and found it locked, but when he pulled hard on the door, it opened. "He must have locked it and it didn't latch. Come on!"

Katie, Cam, and John slipped out the door. They crept to the backside of the building even though the walkway was in the front. They counted on the police coming in that way.

At the back of the building, they listened for any voices. When they didn't hear anyone, Katie gave them a signal to follow her. Crouching down low, the boys followed her lead.

Cam saw they were heading away from the main path to the castle. He thought it made sense to head to the chapel area where the tunnel had been.

They got to the old metal doors hiding the tunnel entrance and found the doors locked. Cam tried to open one of the doors, but it didn't move. John got on one door while Cam was on the other and they both shook them. Luckily, the boys were able to force the doors open.

Katie was sorry that neither ghost was there to help them unlock the gates or guide them through the tunnels like before. She knew it was all on her now. She hoped to guide the boys through the tunnels to the elevator shaft. She also hoped they wouldn't run into Lupu.

It was hard to keep their voices down while they were going through the tunnel. All of them, at some point, hit their heads on the uneven ceiling. At one spot, their lights upset a group of bats that flew right toward them.

They ducked down to the ground while waving their hands around to scare the bats. It worked and the bats flew right by them.

Katie hadn't run into bats when she was in the tunnel before with Anna guiding her. But this time, Anna wasn't there. Katie wished Anna would be there with her now. She couldn't worry about that, so she stopped wishing and paid attention to where she was going.

Finally, their phone lights lit up the base of the old shaft. Katie saw the ancient elevator car inside the metal rails. In this light, it looked like some kind of ride at Disneyland, but she knew the difference; this one involved real danger.

The boys waved their lights all around, trying to see what was around them. John shined his light up the shaft. "Dang! Are we going to have to climb that?" He couldn't see the end of the shaft.

"You don't have to, but I hope you won't make me go alone," she said. She knew she shouldn't have said that. It just came out. She knew Cam, and even John would always be in for an adventure like this.

"We're going," Cam said. "How did you get up there last time?" he asked.

"You see, over there, against the wall? There's a ladder. It's bolted on," she said.

"That can't be safe," John said, as their three lights shone on it.

"That's because it isn't," Katie said, with a slight smirk on her lips. "Oh, and watch out for the rust, some of it is pretty sharp." She felt pretty tough at that point. She hoped she could stay that way.

UPSTAIRS

Chapter 43

Ruth woke up to total darkness. Trying to move, she realized she was bound and gagged. She tried to make some noise, but it was no use. The old door and walls of the closet muted any sounds she could make. *I guess I'm still inside the closet*, she thought. *There aren't too many other places I could be.* Ruth worried about being too loud. She didn't want Lupu to come back and do something more desperate to keep her quiet.

Lupu wasn't near the closet. He and Radu had gone down a level to the music room to find the gold. He tried pulling on the firebox, but it didn't budge. Although no longer in the *Securitate*, he still had some strong observation skills. He remembered having seen Katie checking the stones in the hidden staircase, so he and Radu went there. They used their lights to improve their search and it paid off. They were able to find the two stones with the faint carvings of the M below a crown. He knew that must identify Queen Marie in some way.

They tried pushing them and found the stones would only move a little, except the firebox area still wouldn't open. Finally, they pushed the stones at the same time. This time when it opened, they heard a click and rushed back up to the fireplace.

The two stood there with their eyes and mouths wide open. They had never seen so much gold. Radu stepped over and picked up handfuls of it. He let it slip through his fingers and then grabbed some more. Lupu saw Radu's lust for the gold, and it confirmed he couldn't trust Radu with any of it.

After getting over the impact of finding so much gold, Lupu told Radu they'd have to hurry up and move it. The two men struggled with the cases. Each man tried to carry one of the chests. After only a moment, they gave up that idea. Next, they decided to each take one side of each chest. Together, it wasn't too difficult for them to move the chests, one at a time. They did have trouble carrying the chests down the narrow steps of the secret staircase. The old wooden chests bumped along the stones. Radu had a tougher time carrying the heavy gold. He wasn't as strong as Lupu, and he struggled to barely hold the chests above the ground. He had to keep refreshing his grip. It took two trips to get both chests to the secret entrance of the elevator shaft.

At the same time the men were moving the chests, Katie and the boys were trying to get up the old elevator shaft. Cam was the first to go up the rusty ladder carefully taking one rung at a time. He expected it to be a little shaky, but he was surprised when it didn't wobble at all. *It's much sturdier than I thought.*

Then, John started up the ladder as soon as Cam got about four or five rungs above John's reach. Katie was the last one up the ladder.

"This isn't too bad," John said to the others. Katie wasn't so sure. She remembered how scared she was the other night going up AND down the ladder. She didn't like it. Still, she knew they couldn't go in through the front door of the castle. The police were sure to stop them.

Before they started up, Katie had shown Cam and John her trick with the light from her phone and how she put it in her shirt pocket. Unfortunately, both boys were wearing t-shirts without pockets. They had to rely on the little bit of light Katie's phone was giving off.

Cam changed from a confident grip on the ladder to wrapping an arm around it as he climbed. All three of the teens were taking each rung one-at-a-time.

Midway up there was a definite lurch in the ladder. "What was that?" John asked.

"Should we keep going?" Katie asked.

"It'll be okay," Cam said. He tried to sound calm, but he, like the others, wasn't really sure.

"Maybe we'd better spread out more on this ladder," Cam called down. "We might have too much weight in one small area for this old ladder to hold."

"Good idea," John said. "I'll let you get a little higher before I start up again. Then, you'll let me get up the ladder some more, okay Katie?"

"Okay," she answered. She didn't mind waiting where she was. It was climbing higher up that felt worse for her.

Cam got around 75 feet high when the ladder gave another lurch. This time, some of the older, rustier bolts flew out of their brackets and fell to the ground with a sharp ping. The shaft echoed with the new sounds of groaning metal. All of Cam's senses shouted to him, *Danger!* Cam felt his heart racing and his hands sweating.

"Hold on!" Cam yelled.

"What's happening?" Katie yelled back.

With that, the whole ladder leaned away from the wall with a nasty creaking sound.

Luckily, they kept their grip on the ladder. They rode it for about four feet as it leaned into the metal rails of the elevator frame. The ladder hitting the rails almost made them fall off. They found themselves halfway on the ladder and halfway on the support pieces of the elevator rails. Everyone screamed. They all grabbed onto whatever metal they could. Then, there was one final lurch of the ladder. Fortunately, it didn't go anywhere. It mostly stayed in place. Katie was never more scared in her life. She couldn't even bring herself to take the phone out of her pocket to use its light.

Cam, still higher up on the ladder, was able to reach into his pocket and pull out his phone. He turned on the light and shined it down. He saw the ladder was against the old metal rails and cross supports. Both John and Katie had one leg and arm on the ladder and one on the supports. The rails still looked solid, but the ladder looked like it was ready to fall down completely. Cam shined his light above his head. The ladder had broken about 15 feet above his head. The section of the ladder they were all on was hanging only by a few bolts that were caught on the steel framework.

"Quick! As smoothly as you guys can, move over to those cross pieces!" he shouted down to John and Katie. He kept the light shining on the weakest part of the ladder. Thankfully they understood.

Both John and Katie carefully put both of their hands on the cross pieces. John and Cam moved their feet first to the rails. When Katie kicked her foot off the ladder, the whole section of ladder they had been on rocked.

It rocked twice, then broke loose and fell into the darkness, all the way to the ground. It made such a terrible noise that they tried to block their ears as best as they could, but it wasn't enough to stop the ringing in their ears.

Inside the castle, Lupu and Radu heard the loud noise. They paused to try to make out what the sound was but had no idea where it was coming from or what caused it. In the elevator shaft, Katie yelled up to Cam and John, "Keep climbing up! That's our best chance. We're closer to the top than the bottom."

"I hope these old pieces of metal hold better than the ladder," Cam said. "I've got an idea. Let's do this one at a time. You guys hold on to where you are, and I'll go up first. Then John, and then you, Katie. That way we won't have so much sideways movement."

"Ok, but don't take too long," Katie cried out.

Cam had to put his phone back in his pocket, but Katie and John took out their phones and shined them up to help Cam see better. "Thanks, that helps a lot," he said. It took a while for Cam to finally make it to the top of the shaft. He was then able to get to the platform and stepped up onto it. "Hey, Katie, where's that metal lever?" Cam yelled down.

"It's up there and to the right of the ladder," Katie replied.

"I'm going to have to get inside before John gets here. This platform isn't big enough for all of us," Cam yelled down.

As John neared the end of his climb, Cam left his phone shining from the edge of the platform. Then, he found the lever and pushed open the door.

There was a heavy thud that neither John nor Katie could hear from inside the shaft.

After about three minutes, John made it to the platform too. He saw how small the platform was, so he also went inside the castle, leaving his phone shining next to Cam's.

Another heavy thud echoed inside the castle, but not inside the shaft.

Katie was last, but with the boys' phones lighting her way, she finally got to stand up on the platform. She was a little annoyed though. She thought they could at least help her up onto the platform. It was only when she stepped through the passageway, she found out why they hadn't helped her.

STILL MORE ROOM IN THE CLOSET
Chapter 44

Katie had all three phones in her hand as she entered the dark room. The lights pointing down to the floor came across Cam and John, both lying on the floor. A strong hand pushed her from behind. She ended up sprawled across Cam and John, but they didn't say a thing. "What?" Katie said.

Both Cam and John lay on the floor, unconscious, but Katie only knew that they didn't respond when she landed on top of them. The sudden fear, *Are they dead?* came to her mind. She tried to look around. Something was holding her down on top of them.

"Do not move or I will do the same to you like your friends here," Lupu warned.

Panicking, Katie asked, "What did you do to them?" She tried to see but couldn't with the phone lights scattered around the floor. Only small parts of the still, dark forms of her friends were visible beneath her.

"Radu, use the tape and put them in with the other girl," Lupu commanded. "You take her too."

Radu left for only a moment or two before coming back with some dark gray tape. He bound Katie's hands and feet, placed a short strip over her mouth, then set her aside. Next, he did the same for the two unconscious boys.

With the help of Lupu, Radu managed to get John slung over his shoulder. He staggered up the stairs. He dumped John down next to Ruth in the closet and shut the door. Lupu carried Cam upstairs while Radu carried Katie. Radu dropped Katie onto the boys who were slumped next to Ruth.

The inside of the closet was as black as ink. Katie didn't know how she'd ever get out of this. She was just glad Lupu hadn't killed her. She lay there motionless for what seemed like at least a minute or two. *Please don't kill me. I don't want to die,* she prayed.

Katie wasn't sure what the next sound was. It was too high a pitch to be either Cam or John. It must be Ruth, she thought. "Ruth!" she tried to say behind the tape over her mouth. Unfortunately, it only came out as, "uuuth!"

"Kkkyyy," came the reply.

Yes, it was Ruth's voice. Katie started to squirm around. Ruth was doing the same thing. Since she couldn't use her hands, Katie felt around with her head, following the sounds made by Ruth. Katie did that until she was pretty sure she could tell where Ruth's head was. And Ruth could tell where Katie was since her eyes were more used to being in the dark closet. She had been in there for a long time.

Katie started moving her mouth across where she thought Ruth's shoulder would be. If I can rub off the edge of my tape, then maybe I can get it to roll back enough to stick to her instead of my mouth, she hoped.

She rubbed her head a few times before the tape started to roll off. It finally caught on Ruth's shoulder. It stuck and pulled away enough for Katie to be able to talk.

"Ruth? Are you ok?" she asked. A muffled sound came back to the affirmative. "Rub the edge of the tape to get it to unstick," Katie told her. Ruth used Katie's shoulder and was able to get the tape mostly off her mouth.

The two girls talked over what to do next. With their extended time in the darkness, their vision increased. Katie tried to feel around for something that she could use to break free from the tape. A rusty old hinge on the inside of the door had an edge that gave Katie some hope. She turned around enough to get her hands by the hinge and started rubbing the tape along the edge. It worked. The tape started to fray apart. Before she knew it, she was able to pull her hands and break the little bit of tape left uncut. After that, it was easy for her to tear the tape off her and Ruth. Together, the two girls unwrapped the tape off the wrists of the still unconscious boys.

The girls tried to wake Cam and John.

LUPU AND RADU

Chapter 45

Lupu and Radu were able to pry open the secret panel they had found hours earlier. They also used their time to tie a rope around each chest of gold. Lupu had come up with the plan to lower the chests down the elevator shaft and then escape that way themselves.

Neither Lupu nor Radu had flashlights. They didn't think to use their phones, mostly because they were busy with the heavy chests and ropes. They dragged one chest to the edge of the platform and slowly lowered it over the side.

It was heavy and they worried the rope might fray or the chest would catch on the ladder. They were happy when the chest went all the way down. Once they felt slack in the first line, they let go of the rope. The next chest was equally as difficult to handle, but they managed to lower that chest, too.

Now it was their turn to escape via the shaft. Before Lupu could start down, Radu leapt onto the platform and stepped onto the first rung of the ladder. Lupu was mad at Radu. *You'd better not be thinking you can take any of the gold before I get there*, Lupu thought. Then, he remembered Radu wouldn't be able to move even one of the chests without his help.

Lupu stepped into the shaft and put his foot on the first rung of the ladder when he heard Radu scream. The bit of light in the shaft from the room showed Radu falling backward into the darkness.

Rushing, due to his greed, Radu hadn't seen the missing rungs of the ladder until it was too late. He didn't have the strength to hold on. He was tired from moving the gold and the tied-up teens. Radu hit the elevator framework a few times, tossed back and forth as he fell. His ankle caught in a metal support just yards from the bottom of the shaft, saving his life. He hung there unmoving and upside-down, with an obviously broken leg.

Lupu's first reaction to Radu's scream was disgust. *That weakling! He couldn't even hang onto a ladder*, Lupu thought. Now with his hands free, Lupu took out his phone to use its light to see more clearly what had happened. His light lit up the broken part of the ladder. He could also make out the form of Radu stuck in the framework. To him, it looked like Radu was dead. Lupu smiled when he was able to make out the two chests of gold resting safely at the bottom of the shaft. *This certainly makes it easier for me. I didn't need to share it with you, Radu. One less witness, too. Hmm, there should be no witnesses. Those kids . . .* he thought.

As he pulled out his knife, he stopped. There was a faint sound, but it wasn't coming from the elevator shaft. He turned his head to the side to hear it better. It was two low tones close together with a pause in between. Then it repeated itself, getting louder.

He stopped for a moment to listen to the sounds. He looked down at the knife in his hand. *It's time to take care of those kids*, he thought. He opened the knife and started up the stone stairs toward the teens.

He got midway up the stairs before the first ghost, Queen Marie, appeared. He heard her before he actually saw her. The sounds thump-thump, thump-thump were pulsating in his ears. He saw the ghost with its heart inside its chest, beating. Now he understood.

The sounds were from the beating heart of the Queen. The thought of a ghost with a heart beating in its chest made Lupu hesitate, but only for a moment. He quickly remembered how much he had to lose. His greed moved him forward. *The ghosts only scared me before because I wasn't ready for them then. Only scary faces and no bodies. This is now, and I will be ready.*

The queen's normally friendly face was gone. It was again the face of a horrible monster as she floated down toward him on the stairs. He charged up the stairs with his knife blade flashing. He plunged it right through the ghostly figure.

"Ha!" he said in his arrogant way. "You tried to scare me?"

He stopped before the top of the stairs and looked back at the ghost. She was still making that horrible face, but she was fading away. She had done all she could, except it was no use against the man who wanted to steal her gold.

Then, a few feet beyond the top of the stairs stood the other ghost, Anna. This ghost was not as easy to see through as she had been before. This ghost had something more to her. Lupu wasn't going to let this one bother him either though. He walked with a deliberate stride up to the top of the stairs and stopped there.

"Get out of my way!" he demanded of the ghost. "I've come to give you some more company. Do you like ghost children?" he asked the ghost teasingly. "I'm going to kill those kids." His eyes were narrow with hate as he waved his knife at Anna.

The next moment, his eyes flew open in surprise. Real arms burst toward him from the ghost. He felt the pressure of hands he hadn't expected on his chest. He stumbled backward and dropped his knife as he tried to grab the rope handrail attached to the wall.

Lupu missed the rope and tumbled backward down the stone stairs with cries of pain. He stopped at the bottom of the staircase. His head was bleeding and he looked as if he might be dead.

At the top of the stairs, with Anna still behind her, Katie stood looking down at Lupu. It was Katie who had rushed through Anna to push him.

Katie saw Inspector Popescu standing at the bottom of the stairs a step or two beyond Lupu. He had seen and heard Lupu's last words. He reached down and put his hand on Lupu's neck, feeling for a pulse.

He nodded to Katie and said, "He is alive. And you? Your arm is bleeding." He pulled out his phone to call for an ambulance.

As the Inspector stood there, Lupu moaned and moved a little, but he was in no condition to put up a fight.

Katie looked down and saw the blood on her arm. Lupu's knife had cut her when she pushed him. Katie's friends appeared behind her.

RETRIEVING THE GOLD
Chapter 46

Inspector Popescu called up to Katie and asked, "Did he get the gold?"

"Almost," Katie said. Still at the top of the stairs, she pointed past the inspector to the opening of the elevator shaft. "He had help."

The inspector turned to where Katie had pointed. Farther along the wall in the next room he could make out the secret door to the elevator shaft. It was open just a crack and if she didn't tell him, he might have missed it entirely. He went to it and poked his head inside, but it was too dark to see anything. He pulled out a small flashlight he kept in his jacket. His light lit up the entire shaft. He saw Radu moving around, still hanging upside-down. He had not been able to free himself. The inspector called down in Romanian, "Don't move. We will be down to get you shortly."

Within a minute, three more police officers came to the bottom of the stone stairs. Inspector Popescu left them with Lupu and came up with a first aid kit one of the officers had brought. He took out a bandage and put it on Katie's arm. "You will be alright, but you were very lucky. Lupu is a dangerous man."

Later, the inspector asked her, "Who was that woman I saw you with up there at the top of the stairs?"

"That was Anna Cristea, my great-great-grandma," Katie answered. "And, of course, the woman on the stairs before was Queen Marie. They are ghosts. We were afraid to tell you that part earlier. We didn't think you'd believe anything we said if we did that."

The inspector put his hand to his chin, with a questioning look on his face. He had to think about that for a while. Before he had a chance to say anything else, Ruth, Cam, and John all started to tell their stories of what happened.

A cry for help coming from the shaft reminded the inspector he must attend to Radu. The inspector wasn't sure how he could get to where Radu was hanging. "How did he get down there?" he asked Katie.

Katie told the inspector about the outside access to the elevator shaft. He hadn't known it was there. "I can show you how to get there," she told him.

"How did you know about it?" he asked. Then, he held up his hand to stop her. "I know, your ghost grandma told you about it." There was doubt in his voice.

"Well, yes," Katie replied, a little embarrassed. "I'll show you. You'll see." By this time, medics and police were all around. Some medics gave aid to Lupu, Cam, and John. Both medics and officers followed Katie and Ruth as they led the inspector to the outside tunnel entrance.

They found the old metal doors exactly as they had left them, closed but unlocked. Katie was able to direct the group through the tunnels. Now they had a lot of light from all the police flashlights. The trek through the tunnels felt much shorter to Katie this time. The extra light helped them to move faster.

At the end of the tunnel, they found Radu dangling upside down by his ankle. His ankle was stuck between two metal crossbars just 10 feet above the ground. He could only move one of his arms. The other looked like it may have broken in the fall.

"You certainly are lucky," the inspector said. "It looks like if you hadn't been caught by your foot, you would have hit the ground and broken your neck."

Radu didn't feel lucky. He was in a lot of pain. The police and medics worked to get him down. One officer took photos of the scene, even some photos of Radu hanging there.

The inspector walked over to the two chests. Both lay there shut, with rope draped over them. An officer rolled up the ropes and set them next to the chests. With gloves on, they opened the chests. The reflected glow from the gold coins filled the entire end of the tunnel.

Katie and Ruth had to stand back while all this was going on to not get in the way of what the police were doing.

It was Ruth who started looking at the old elevator car sitting within its rails at the bottom of its shaft. On the other side of it, she noticed something was out of place within the dirt, steel, and rock. There, standing on its edge, was a folded piece of paper. It was only partly showing behind a section of steel. "What's that?" Ruth asked Katie.

"Katie walked over and with a sound of glee, said, "It's my letter! Inspector, it's my letter!"

The inspector took it in his gloved hands and carefully unfolded it. Katie and Ruth stood by, impatiently, waiting for him to say something. Finally, he turned to them and said, "Yes, it is your letter, and it is your gold. It lists the exact number of coins we took from you. It even has a royal seal."

Katie let out a sigh of relief. The inspector let Ruth take a photo of the paper while he held it open. He asked the girls not to touch it yet. "It might be used in some way as evidence, so we will need to hold on to it for a while."

Katie was disappointed, but she had grown to trust the inspector and Ruth had some photos of it now. "Do you still need us here? We'd like to get back upstairs. We need to check on Cam and John," Katie said.

The girls passed the medics taking Lupu down the hill from the castle in a stretcher. Police were on both sides of the stretcher. Up in the music room, the girls found Cam and John sitting on the floor leaning against a wall. They both had ice packs on their heads, and there was a medic standing nearby. "They will be OK. Both must go to hospital . . . watched over night," the medic said in broken English.

"*Mulţumim*," Katie said.

Nodding his head, the young medic smiled and said, "You are welcome."

Katie and Ruth walked over and sat down next to Cam and John. "You won't believe what happened while you guys were napping," Katie said. Both boys gave a look of surprise.

"Napping? I wish!" Cam said. Katie and Ruth giggled. Cam and John tried to laugh too. They only managed to get out a "heh" before it hurt too much to go any further with the joke.

Katie and Ruth filled the guys in on what happened after they were knocked out. Ruth filled in the story with what happened in the tunnels with the police. Katie wanted to tell the boys about the letter, but since Ruth was the one to find it, she let her tell them. Ruth pulled out her phone to show them the picture of the letter, but before she could, the medics came over.

"We're happy for you," John said as the medics helped him and Cam stand up. As they walked near the shaft entrance, John leaned in to get one last peek. To be safe, Ruth held on to him. "Oh my gosh! Cam, you have no idea how close we came to dying on that ladder. It completely fell away and it's so deep. You can see it now with all the lights on down there."

Ruth pulled him away from the entrance and back into the room. Cam said, "I'll take your word for it. My head is spinning." Katie took Cam's arm, and the two girls walked their friends down and out of the castle. Both Cam and John enjoyed the attention from the girls. At the bottom of the hill, John said, "I suppose the *clătite* shop is closed." They chuckled.

REMEMBERING THE PAST
Chapter 47

The next few days went by slowly. The pace of the classroom seemed a bit dull to the teens after all they had gone through at Bran Castle. They spent a lot of that time talking with each other about their recent adventure. They were happy with the way things turned out, but they were also sad that their time in Romania was coming to an end.

Before class that last day, the four received notes to meet in Mrs. Popescu's office instead of going to class. Katie hoped she would finally hear about the gold that she had found for her great-great-grandma. Katie wasn't too surprised when Inspector Popescu and his wife welcomed the four friends as they walked into the office.

The Inspector spoke first. "This is not just a matter of finding gold coins. You discovered an important part of Romania's past, one that was hidden for many years. There are many things in our country's past that we want to move on from, but not all of them. You've brought an important part of our history back to us. The discovery of the Dacian gold and its return to the Romanian people is a valuable connection to our ancient Dacian beginnings."

Katie told him, "It was our pleasure. I have come to love this country more than ever. I only knew a little about my family's Romanian background, but now I've learned so much more about it and gotten to meet some wonderful people."

The Inspector added, "I also want you to know, we found that Lupu had a boat rented at Constanța. It's a beach resort at the Black Sea. It's only a four hour car ride from Brașov. He was going to take the gold there first. Then, he planned to take the gold by boat to Turkey and hide there. He would have gotten away with it if you hadn't stopped him," the Inspector said to Katie.

"We all stopped him," Katie replied.

"Yeah, John and I were able to slow him down by letting him knock us out cold. Then, he had to take the time to take us upstairs to lock us in a closet," Cam joked modestly.

"Hey, and I never did get another chance to get my *clătite*," John added with a smile.

"Well, you still have some time," the Inspector said.

"Seriously, Katie, you deserve all the credit," Cam said to Katie. "If it wasn't for you, no one would have found the gold."

"If anything, we all deserve it, especially you and John for coming here with me. And, Ruth, too. It's been so crazy. I came here to know more about my Romanian relatives, and wow, I never expected to meet any of them," Katie said.

"Allow me to get back to your relatives, Katie," Inspector Popescu said. "We can finally honor the wishes of our beloved queen, Marie. The letters we found with the gold have been authenticated, so the Romanian government considers them to be the actual wishes of Queen Marie.

In one letter, Queen Marie wrote that the gold in the two large chests is to be used only for the people of Romania. The coins will be examined, and a current value determined. But for now, I can say the value of those two chests is enormous.

And, as you already know, the smaller chest containing 200 gold Dacian pieces also had a letter from Queen Marie to your great-great-grandmother, Anna Cristea. So, you will be receiving the queen's gift, on behalf of your family."

Katie's heart swelled with pride. She couldn't wait to let her grandma and parents know.

Then Mrs. Popescu added, "Also, I reached out to a teacher here. She looked into the past of Anna Cristea. Here is the information she came up with," she said as she handed Katie a piece of paper. "I thought you might like to have this." Katie looked over the paper. Katie's eyes grew wide as she read what was written on it.

"This is awesome. This lists Anna's parents and grandparents, what they did for a living, and where they lived. It shows when and where she was married, when she went to America . . ." Katie couldn't hold back her tears of joy. She was so excited to get all this information. No one in her family had ever known this much about Anna. She valued this information more than the queen's gift of gold.

"Oh, my gosh. Thank you, thank you so much. We never knew all this. I can't wait to tell my mom and my grandma. They'll be so excited about it. I can't thank you enough," Katie said.

"Please, it is my pleasure. I have a co-worker who knew exactly where to go to get this information," Mrs. Popescu said. "But, I . . .," Mrs. Popescu didn't have a chance to finish saying what she started. Katie was so excited and cut her off.

Without waiting, Katie said, "It's fantastic. Oh, I do have one more thing to ask of you, if you don't mind. Would you be able to translate the Queen's note? It's all in Romanian. Katie turned to Ruth. "You haven't shared the picture of the Queen's letter with me yet."

Ruth pulled up the photo of the letter on her phone and passed it to the teacher. Katie could hardly wait while the teacher looked at the letter.

"It says, 'My dearest friend Anna. Thank you for your friendship during my days at Castle Bran. I deeply feel the guilt of bringing you and your husband into the dangers that were responsible for such sorrow in your young life. Still, I know you will keep our secret safe as you start again in your new country.

I want you to know our visits together here at Bran have meant the world to me. Our talks helped me many times to see there is still good in people even in difficult situations. Those around me often only seek my influence for their benefit while some try to control me. You have been the exact opposite - a light in the darkness to this traveler in life. I hope you will accept these 200 coins as a small token of my esteem. Please use this for yourself, your family, or in any way you see fit. (signed) Marie.'

"Wow. So cool," John said.

"It's awesome," Cam said. "How many people can say a Queen wrote to their family and gave them a gift of gold? Or, that they were friends with a queen? It sounds like your great-great-grandma was very special."

"Yeah, a lot like you," Katie said with a blush on her face. Her words brought a quick smile to Cam's face.

"But, there's more," Mrs. Popescu was able to say.

FAMILY
TREE

FILLING IN A FEW BLANKS

Chapter 48

"Katie, you didn't let me tell you the rest. I am a history teacher, as well as a language teacher. So, I was interested in knowing more about Anna myself. I found some things, but you have to hear about the Queen and the King first.

Just before the death of her husband, King Ferdinand, Queen Marie's son decided that he didn't want to become a king. So her son left Romania, and that put a lot of pressure on Marie.

But after three years, her son changed his mind and returned to Romania. He then wanted to become the King."

"I'll bet the Queen was happy," Katie said.

"Only at first. Unfortunately for Marie, he no longer liked his mother. He took away all her power. He cut her off from her life as Queen. He looked for support from a dangerous group called the Iron Guard. It seems that he was afraid she could be seen as being more powerful than him. He knew she was more liked by the people than he was."

"What a jerk!" John said.

"Well, yes, I believe that's how you would say it in English," Mrs. Popescu said with a smile on her face. "That's when Marie left her royal life and spent more time at Bran Castle. That's also when she met Anna. Anna worked in the tea house that was just outside the castle. There were few people the queen could trust at that time. Her son kept Marie away from all of her friends who could have helped her. I'm sure the queen was happy to have found someone she could trust."

"Yes, I saw a picture of the Queen at the tea house, and Anna was in the picture too!" Katie said. "The picture is there in the dining room in the castle. I was able to take a picture of it with my phone after your husband arrested Lupu."

"Yes, I have seen that old photograph," Mrs. Popescu said. "I never knew who the other woman was in the photo, until now."

"I'm glad the Queen had Anna as a friend to talk with," Katie said. "It's important to have friends you can count on." As she said this, she looked at Cam, then John and Ruth. They smiled.

"Katie," Mrs. Popescu said, "you can be proud of Anna. Actually, there is still more to tell you. Queen Marie loved to write. She wrote almost every day about the things that happened in her life. She made them into books. In one of those books, I found where she wrote about Anna."

"Are you kidding?" Katie asked.

"No. She wrote that Anna married and had a daughter, Victoria. She wrote that Anna and her husband, Ion, planned to leave Romania to go to the United States. They wanted to make a better life for themselves and their child. Sadly, Anna's husband died before they could leave Romania. The Queen wrote that she was afraid the Iron Guard might have been involved in Ion's death.

Anna was a strong woman. She took her daughter and went to the United States anyway. She wrote a letter to the Queen after she arrived in America. Anna's letter made Queen Marie very happy. That's when Marie decided to give Anna the gold as a present. But the Queen never got the chance to give Anna the gold. Marie died before she could send it."

"Oh, that's so sad," Ruth said.

"What about the other chests of gold?" John asked. "Why did no one else ever know about them being there in the castle."

"From what I could find out," Mrs. Popescu said, "the queen discovered the gold hidden in Bran Castle and didn't want her son to use it to buy his way into favor with the Iron Guard. Marie wanted it to go to helping the Romanian people. So, she needed someone to help move it for her into a new hiding place. Anna and her husband probably moved the gold and that was their secret.

It was surely the Iron Guard who killed Anna's husband. Trying to get him to tell where the gold was, they would stop at nothing. If Anna thought the Iron Guard killed her husband, she probably left for America to keep her daughter safe," Mrs. Popescu said.

"And," Katie added, "if the Queen had asked Anna to not tell anyone about the chests of gold, I'll bet she didn't even tell her brother. He probably never knew that part of Anna's story to pass along to Victoria."

"So, when the Queen died, the secret was left only to Anna," Mrs. Popescu finished.

"And when Anna died," Katie said, "the secret died with her." Katie, deep in thought, shook her head a few times, with her lips firmly closed. She was thinking of how much her family never knew, until now. This had all been so much for Katie to take in. She felt her head spinning with information that she had always wanted to know. "It's going to take me a little while for all this to sink in." Katie cleared her head with a quick shake. "I can't thank you enough for all you've done for me and my family. I'm sure Anna would thank you too."

"It was my pleasure," Mrs. Popescu said. "I have always been interested in history and the life of Queen Marie. The Queen and Anna were amazing role models for all women. They saw what they wanted to do and did it. You're the same way."

After a few moments of silence, both Mr. and Mrs. Popescu stood. Mrs. Popescu said, "That's all we have for you. You all probably want to start packing for your trip home and saying your goodbyes to your fellow students.

John and Ruth were the first to leave the office heading for the dorms. Katie and Cam walked a few yards behind. Katie tugged at the back of Cam's shirt and he stopped and turned towards her. John and Ruth kept walking, not knowing their friends had stopped. Katie looked into Cam's eyes.

"Thank you for being here with me. There's no one else I'd rather be here with," Katie said.

"I wouldn't want to be anywhere else," Cam replied. He leaned forward and softly gave Katie a kiss.

Katie knew this was one of the best days of her life. She gave Cam a long, tight hug and Cam hugged her back, just as tightly.

TIME TO GO BACK HOME
Chapter 49

Ruth was the first of the four to start the long trip back home. Katie and Cam said their goodbyes to Ruth at the dorm. They each hugged her and promised to keep in contact. John had taken longer to say his goodbyes. He and Ruth went for a walk earlier that morning near the dorm. Fortunately, their goodbyes were more like, "see you soon," according to John. He had talked with his parents, and they decided to go to England for Christmas break. John's mom always wanted to visit the quaint, snowy, Christmas villages in England. Plus, the two planned to be seeing each other through the internet on a regular basis.

Ruth's cab arrived at the dorm disappointingly on time. She was sharing the taxi ride to the airport with two other girls from England. John helped by putting Ruth's bags into the taxi's trunk. The sadness everyone felt was clearly seen on their faces. Ruth saw this and wanted to cheer up her new friends.

So, she went back to the trunk and pulled out a scarf from her suitcase. She wrapped it around her neck. With style, she threw the loose end over her shoulder and blew them a kiss before getting back in the car.

Katie broke out in a huge smile when she saw Ruth put on the scarf. She recognized it as the scarf Ruth brought with her to knit. "What a nice guy, John. You finished that for her, didn't you?" Katie asked.

John blushed a little and said, "Somebody had to."

In spite of Ruth's little joke, the three friends sadly watched their newest friend drive off.

Katie turned to Cam and said, "I'm really glad I don't have to say goodbye to you."

"I know what you mean," Cam said as he took her hand in his. Cam continued to hold Katie's hand as the teens went back up to their dorm rooms to get their things together. They were going to be leaving later that afternoon themselves.

Cam and John hadn't even started packing, so they went off to pack. Katie had already finished packing her things, so she decided to take the time to call her parents.

Her room felt so empty without Ruth there. Katie knew talking to her family would cheer her up, and she had a lot she needed to tell them. They put her on speakerphone.

Katie's dad told her that her grandma spoke with someone from the Romanian government earlier. They made a deal. The Romanian government will keep the gold coins and pay Katie's grandma their value in US dollars. "It was quite a lot of money," her dad said.

As they talked more, Katie glanced down at the note she had gotten about Anna. Without thinking, she found herself looking out the window. Outside, clouds moved in. She could see herself reflected in the window glass. As she and her family continued to talk, she saw the reflection showed the room growing darker. She felt the familiar cold blast and before she knew it, she was seeing Anna and the Queen reflected as well.

Katie's mom said on the phone, "Katie, are you sure this is a good time to talk? It sounds like someone is trying to talk to you. I heard a woman say something like 'thank you' in Romanian."

"You did, Mom. It was Queen Marie," Katie told her.

"Yeah, right," her mom replied.

"No, Olga," Katie's grandma said. "I heard a voice saying, *mulțumim pentru toți, și la revedere.* That means 'we' thank you a lot and goodbye. Then, I heard her call you something I call you all the time, *"Nepoata mea dragă,* my darling granddaughter."

"You both heard right," Katie said with a tear falling down her cheek. Katie looked up. The queen had left. Anna was still there. A tear, barely visible, was making its way down her smiling, fading face. Anna's ghost reached her hand toward Katie's chin. She held it for a brief moment and gave Katie's cheek a gentle pat. Then, Anna was gone.

Later in the conversation, Katie's grandma said she wanted to share the gold with Katie and the others as well. Her dad said the money would help cover the cost of college for Katie and her three friends. Katie decided to let her parents tell her friends the good news after everyone got home. Her heart filled with joy when she heard her grandma say she'd like to visit Romania. Maybe they would make it a family trip very soon. Katie reached up to gently touch the pendant on her necklace. Yes, Grandma, and you can wear your necklace when we come back to Romania together, she thought.

For a moment, the silence of the room felt like an enormous weight dropped onto Katie. The tears were starting to run down Katie's face now. She didn't know why, but she felt she'd never see Queen Marie or Anna again. In her heart, she also understood the queen had stayed to make sure the gold was found and given to her beloved country to help her people. Anna had stayed to make sure her family finally got the queen's gift. Both were freed from their duties to the people they loved. They could rest now. Katie never thought she could feel so empty at the loss of people she never knew, but her loss was filled with an equal amount of happiness for the new friends she'd come to love.

THE END (For now)

Romanian / English Translations
used in the book

Romanian Words	Pronunciation Guide	English Words
Afară	Ah-far-ah	Outside
Ai venit	Eye venn-eat	You came
Aici	Eye-eech	Here
Aici a fost depusă în anul 1940. Inima Reginei Maria a României	Eye-eech ah fost de-puz-ah un an-newl 1940 in-i-ma rey-gin-eh mar-ee-ah ah ro-man-ee-ah	Here was deposited in 1940 the heart of Queen Marie of Romania
Aurul dacic	Ow-rule dah-cheek	Dacian gold
Aurul tău e aici	Ow-rule tah-ye eye-eech	Your gold is here
Bani	Bah-n	Money
Bună	Boo-nah	Good day (used like "Hello")
Bună studenți	Boo-nah stew-dents	Hello students
Bună ziua	Boo-nah zee-u-ah	Good day
Bunică	Boo-knee-kah	Grandmother
Căminul	Ca-me-newl	Dorms
Clătite	Kla-tee-tay	Crepe (a pancake like pastry)

Da	Daw	Yes
Dacians	Dah-chi-ans	Dacians
Domnul	Dome-newll	Mr.
Dragă	Draw-gah	Dear
Dragă ai venit din nou	Draw-gah eye venn-eet deen no	Dear, you came again
Drum Bun	Droom-boon	Safe travels
Faceți nimic	Fah-chets nim-eek	Do nothing
Familia	Fam-ill-ee-ah	Family
Hallo. Ești bine?	Hall-low. Yes-te-bee-nee	Hello. Are you well?
Inspector de poliție	In-spec-tore-ool deh poe-lets-see-ya	Inspector of police
Mămăligă	Mama-lee-gah	Polenta
Mulțumim	Mool-sue-meme	We thank you
Ne pare rău dar trebuie să pleci. Este ora închiderii.	Neh par-rey rau dar tray-bouy-yeh se play-ch. Yes-tey or-ah un-chee-der-ey	I am sorry, but you must leave. It is closing time.
Nepoată	Neh-po-at-a	Granddaughter
Nepoata mea dragă	Neh-po-at-a may-ah draw-gah	My darling granddaughter
Noi dorim să mergem apoi la Brașov	Noy door-eem sah mare-gem ap-oy la bra-shov	We want to go back to Brașov
Nu mulțumesc	New mool-sue-mesk	No, thank you
Nu pleca	New play-kah	Don't leave

Numele tău de familie este Cristea?	Noom-eh-leh tau deh fam-ill-ee-ah yes-te christ-ee-ah	Is your family name (last name) Cristea?
Opriți	Oh-pre-tse	Stop
Plecați	Play-cah-tz	Leave
Salut. Bine ai venit	Sa-lute bee-ney eye veh-neet	Hello. Welcome
Stai	Sty	Stay
Stai acolo! Poliția	Sty ah-col-oh poe-lets-see-ya	Stay there. Police
Stați	Statz	Stay
Studentă	Stew-dent-tah	(female) student
Sunt bine	Soon-t bee-ney	I am fine
Tu ai colierul meu	Two eye co-lee-air-ool may-ow	You have my necklace
Vlad Țepes	Vlad sep-ish	Vlad Țepes
Vrăjitoare	Rah-gee-to-wa-ray	Witch

Discussion Questions

1. Does Katie usually make good or bad choices in this story? Find at least 3 examples as evidence for your answers.

2. How do you think this story would change if it was told from Cam's point of view?

3. How did Katie, Cam, and John change from the beginning of the story to the end.

4. What might be a different ending for this story that you think would work as well, or better than its ending.

5. If you had to change the title of this book, what would you change it to?

Heart of the Castle:

The True Facts

Romania

Romania is located in Eastern Europe. It is bordered by the Black Sea, the countries of Bulgaria, Hungary, Moldova, Serbia, and the Ukraine. It's about the size of the state of Oregon in the United States.

Transylvania

Transylvania is an area within Romania. Shown in white on this map, it covers much of central and northwestern Romania.

Brief History (Dacians, Romans, Knights, Rulers)

Back in the year 100 AD, the area of Romania was called Dacia and ruled by people called the Dacians. They were a wealthy society and had a great deal of gold. The Romans, who had a strong army at that time, wanted to control the area of Dacia. So, the Romans brought their armies to Dacia and killed many of the Dacians and tried to take their gold.

The **Dacians** were able to hide much of their wealth in the mountains of the area that is now called Transylvania. The Dacian empire ended around the year 275AD.

(**Teutonic Knights** were crusaders who put together an army in order to protect pilgrims, who were traveling within the Holy Lands (Middle East) and the Baltic (the countries of Estonia, Latvia, and Lithuania) to pray and show signs of respect.)

There are rumors that some of that gold made its way to the **Teutonic Knights**, who in 1212 occupied the area that later became **Bran Castle** as a stronghold. The Knights may have hidden the found gold in the castle, saving it there for a future time of need. Before it was ever used, the castle changed hands several times and the knowledge of the gold's existence, along with its location within the castle, were lost to time.

After the Roman Empire (1500 to 1806), the control of Transylvania came under the Austrian Empire (1814 to 1867). That was followed by the Austro-Hungarian Empire (1867 to 1918). During this 51 year period, the Hungarian portion of this empire controlled all of Transylvania. After World War I, the area of Transylvania was given back to the Romanians.

Bran Castle

The people of Transylvania first built Bran in 1337. King Louis I of Hungary gave them permission to build it. Its purpose was to stop the expansion of the Ottoman Empire into that area. The Ottoman Empire started in the country of Turkey and spread out under their Islamic ruled government throughout the Middle East and Eastern Europe.

Each time the Ottomans went into Western Europe, they had to go through Romania. In order to defend their towns, many cities built fortified walls around them.

Those walls can still be seen today around Romanian cities like Sibiu, Alba-Julia, Brașov, and Sighișoara.

Bran Castle was restored several times to serve as a fortress, most recently in the 1880s, but it fell into disrepair after that. Then, in 1920 the castle was given to Queen Marie of Romania.

She had the castle restored. She and her husband used it as a summer home throughout the rest of her lifetime.

This castle which is now commonly known as "Dracula's Castle" actually never belonged to the person known as Dracula. Vlad Țepes was the ruler of Wallachia, a portion of modern day Romania, and had an army. Vlad's nickname was Dracula. In English, Dracula means 'little devil'. Vlad Țepes was known to be a cruel person, quick to put people to death. Though feared by most, he is credited by some with keeping Romania safe from invasions by the Ottoman Empire. Vlad's only real connection to Bran Castle was that he was held captive there for a few months in 1462.

Bran Castle has been modified through the years, but it has 5 levels. Under Bran Castle, there are 12,500 passageways, and 15 miles of tunnels.

Section of city wall entrance in Alba-Julia

Bran Castle Floor Plan

- 1st Level -

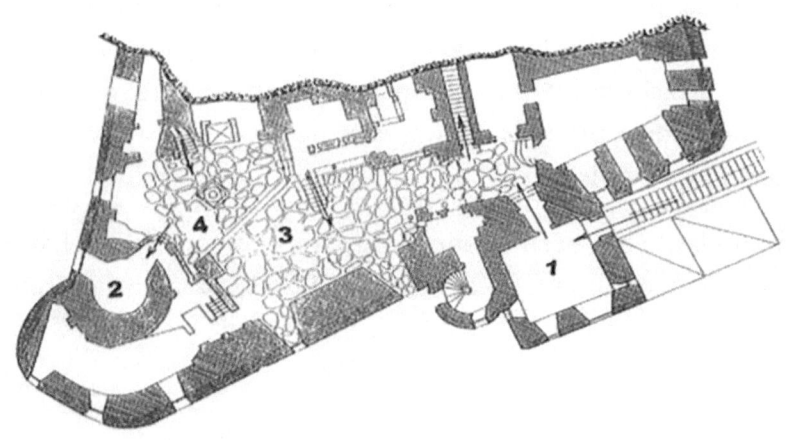

1. Guard room
2. Prince Mircea's Chapel
3. Inner courtyard
4. The fountain capital

Bran Castle Floor Plan

– 2nd Level –

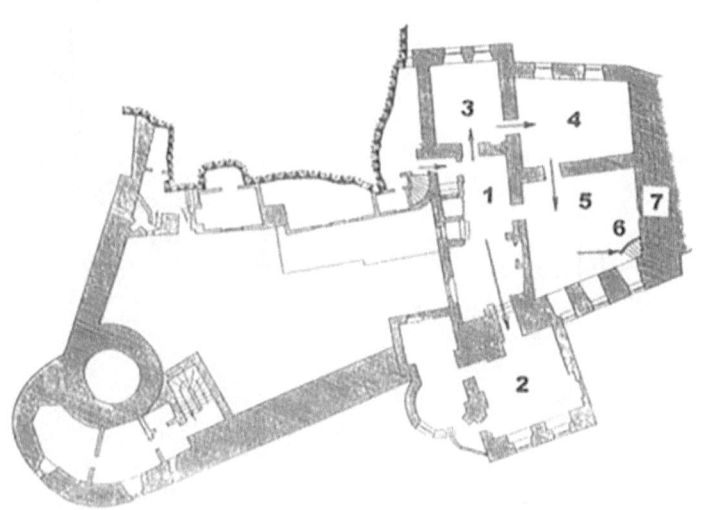

1. Hall

2. Queen Maria's bedroom

3. Passage room

4. Gothic Hall – Yellow Hall

5. Great Hall

6.-7. Secret staircase

Bran Castle Floor Plan
– 3rd Level –

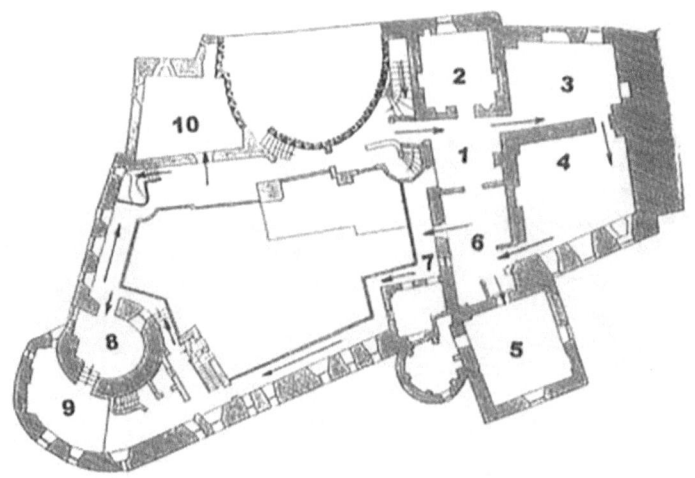

1. Crossing room
2. Biedermeier Hall
3. King Ferdinand's bedroom
4. Dining room
5. Costume Hall
6. Crossing room
7. Interior Corridor
8.-9. Green Bedroom
10. Screening room

Bran Castle Floor Plan
– 4th Level –

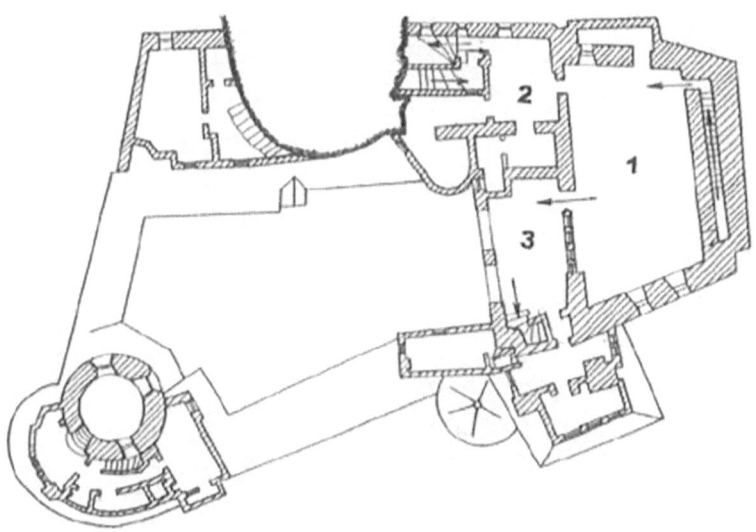

1. Music Hall, open hall space, game room, study, Balcony, and Library
2. The anteroom of the music hall
3. The loggia

Bran castle floor plan
- 5th level -

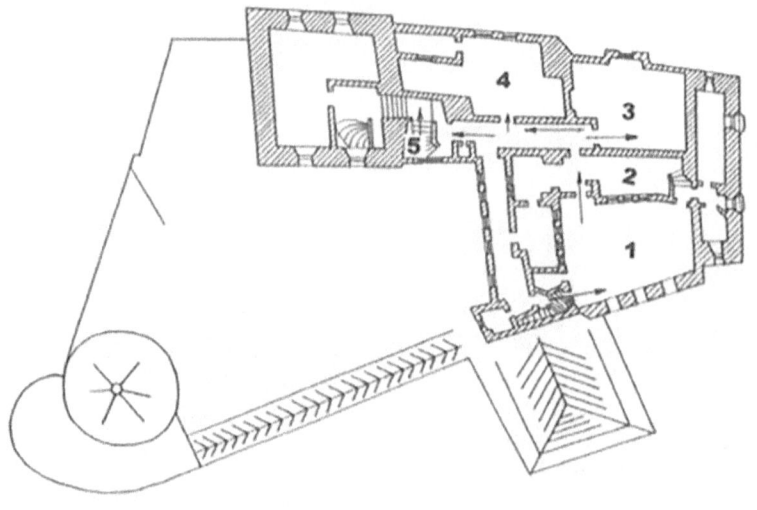

1-3-4. Prince Nicolae's Apartment

2. Access to the East Tower

5. Main Stairs

6. Bran Castle Terrace

Queen Marie of Romania

(born 1875 – died 1938)

Marie was the daughter of the Duke and Duchess of Edinburgh; the granddaughter of England's Queen Victoria. She married Ferdinand I in 1893 in an arranged marriage. Ferdinand's father was King Carol I of Romania. Ferdinand became the King of Romania when his father died in 1914, and kept that title until his death in 1927.

Though the people of Romania liked King Ferdinand, they loved Marie. She dedicated her life to Romania and its people. During the first World War, Marie worked as a nurse to wounded Romanian soldiers.

Marie also played a major role in getting lands returned that had been taken away from Romania. Even though Marie was born in England, she immersed herself in Romanian culture and promoted Romania to the rest of the world. She often wore the sewn (embroidered) peasant blouses. She became someone the average Romanian could identify with.

Example of a typical peasant blouse from the Transylvanian Region.

Also, as Queen, Marie made herself available to all people. Marie once said, "My doors were hospitably open to every visitor." She would meet anyone who came to see her, not just people who held high offices in the government.

With Ferdinand's death, Marie's son, Carol II, turned down the prospect of being King, so the throne went to Carol's son, Michael. Later, in 1930, Carol changed his mind and was able to take back the throne.

Unfortunately for Marie, Carol didn't take any advice from his mother and worked at cutting her out of the politics of Romania completely. During those years, Marie spent more time at her two retreats: Bran Castle and Balchik Palace on the Black Sea.

While at Bran, Queen Marie restored much of the castle. She even had electricity brought in and installed an elevator in the empty water well shaft. Marie used the elevator to go from the castle down to outside the castle grounds.

At Bran, Queen Marie's apartment included a hallway, a dressing room, two living rooms, a bedroom, a bathroom, and a dining room.

The Queen's Heart

Queen Marie loved her country and its people. She knew that when she died, her body would be buried in a church where her husband and other Romanian royalty were buried. She asked that after her death her heart be buried at her palace on the Black Sea, in Balchik. At the time of her death the area belonged to Romania.

In 1940, that area of Romania became part of Bulgaria, so Romania moved her heart to Bran Castle where it was placed in a chapel in the hillside below Bran Castle. It stayed there for

31 years before it was moved to the National History Museum. In 2015, it was moved to its current resting place, the Summer Palace at Ploiesti, Romania.

Romanians Coming to America

Coming to America was never easy for the Romanian people. In the early 1900s, people were free to leave the country, but it was expensive to travel and took a long time. Commercial airplane travel did not exist. People had to take ships to cross the Atlantic Ocean. But first, Romanians had to take trains to ports where transatlantic ships would leave from.

My grandmother left Romania to live in the United States in the early 1900s. The trip from Romania to the United States started with a 2 day train ride to get to a ship sailing to America.

Once at sea, it took a week and a half to arrive in New York harbor. She was traveling by herself, so she had to find a family that would say she was their daughter (often young women traveling alone were not allowed into the country). Once in New York City, she had to find a place to live and get a job. She didn't speak English so she worked in a German restaurant while she started to learn English.

After 1947, during the days of Communist rule in Romania, few people were allowed to leave the country. Some left by escaping across the Danube River, while others, who had a way to get American money, bought their way out by bribing (paying) officials for exit visas. People who tried to escape Romania risked their lives or were put in prison.

Romanian Government

Romania had Kings and Queens from 1881 until World War II. Shortly after that time, Romania became part of the

"Eastern Bloc" of socialist countries, which were similar to communistic rule.

After their revolution in 1989, Romania became a democratic republic. Romania's political framework is a semi-presidential representative democratic republic where the Prime Minister is the head of government while the President represents the country internationally.

Securitate

In addition to a more common city police force, Communist Romania had a secret police force. The Romanian name for their secret police was the Securitate. They were the kind of secret police who were known to come to someone's home in the night and take them away without any explanation. The people taken away were often never seen again. These secret police reported to Romania's President, Nicolae Ceaușescu, starting around 1965. They were in place until the revolt against the communist party in December of 1989. After the revolt, the group was disbanded. At one time, this secret group had approximately 25,000 0ffcers and 750,000 informants. The Securitate was responsible for enforcing state rules limiting the media, the right to openly disagree with the government, and freedom of speech. The informants were people willing to tell the authorities of any acts of social disobedience that they knew of. Social disobedience included even innocent acts such as having relatives who lived abroad, studying foreign languages, or even just telling jokes involving the government.

While visiting Romania during this time, I personally experienced Romanians inviting me to their home, but warning me not to say anything until we got inside. They were afraid their neighbors might report them to the police. I was told that Romanians could be fined a month's wages for having a foreigner stay in their home without notifying the police.

The police required citizens to tell them who was visiting and what their conversations were about. In addition to wanting to control what the Romanian people heard, the government wanted people visiting from other countries to pay for hotel rooms using money from those countries. That way, foreign money (also known as 'western currency') was collected by the Romanian government.

The Romanian government used that 'western currency' to pay back money they owed from their part in World War II, also known as war debt.

Summer School in Romania

Romania has several summer school courses available to foreign students. The courses are mostly designed for students to learn the Romanian language, but there are also other activities to help the students learn about the local culture. The summer courses I attended were held at universities, and the students stayed in the university dorms. I attended classes in both the cities of Brașov and Cluj-Napoca, and had a wonderful experience each time, becoming friends with students from around the world.

The schools have changed somewhat since I attended during the Communist era. Today, students are housed in hotels. At the time of writing, the costs in Brașov for 60 hours of language classes are 1,200 Euros (or about $1,400 US dollars) for double occupancy at a 3-star hotel. Students must be at least 18 years old.

Reference Sources

Bran Castle. 3 July 2019. *Britannica School*, Encyclopedia Britannica, school.eb.com/levels/high/article/Bran-Castle/629779. Accessed 15 October 2020.

Lungescu, Oana. *The day I read my secret police file*. The Independent, 2009. *Independent*, www.independent.co.uk. Accessed 2021.

"Ottoman Empire." *Ottoman Empire*, history.com, 3 November 2017, history.com. Accessed 2021.

Schudel, Matt. "Iulian Vlad, head of Romania's secret police during 1989 revolution, dies at 86." *Iulian Vlad, head of Romania's secret police during 1989 revolution, dies at 86*, 30 September 2017, https://www.washingtonpost.com/local/obituaries/iulian-vlad-head-of-romanias-secret-police-during-1989-revolution-dies-at-86/2017/09/30/293cf23e-a5ee-11e7-ade1-76d061d56efa_story.html.

Photo credits

Alba-Julia walled fortifications - R. Fulleman - 1978

Bran Castle (Aerial View): https://designlike.com/dracula-bran-castle-amazing-gothic-arhitectural-design/

Bran Castle (Distance view) by David Stanley https://www.flickr.com

Bran Castle secret staircase (Interior View): By Alessio Damato - Self-photographed, CC BY-SA 3.0, https://commons.wikimedia.org/w/index.php?curid=1147758

Bran Castle secret staircase (Lower entrance): By Ihorpa - Own work, CC BY-SA 3.0, https://commons.wikimedia.org/w/index.php?curid=28336043

Bran Castle secret staircase (Upper entrance): By Ihorpa - Own work, CC BY-SA 3.0, https://commons.wikimedia.org/w/index.php?curid=28336052

Queen Marie - https://upload.wikimedia.org

Romanian peasant blouse - R. Fulleman - 2021

*Special thanks to Castelul Bran (24 General Traian Moșoiu St., Bran, Brașov, Romania, 507025 - www.bran-castle.com) for their permission to use their floor plans of Bran Castle in this book.

Author Bio

Author R. Fulleman has previously written four books: The Ron and Bob Stories (*Limo for Two?*, *Stink Bombs*, and *The Tattoo*), a Hi/Lo book series written at a 2nd grade reading level to offer challenged readers stories that they can gain confidence in their reading abilities. His fourth book, *Faces in the Flames: A Ghost Story*, is the first in a trilogy ghost book series. Look for the third book to this ghost series to be published soon.

R. Fulleman is an identical twin who grew up in the San Fernando Valley in Southern California. He currently lives in Santa Clarita with his wife, enjoying their children and grandchildren.

Author R. Fulleman with his daughter, Suzie în Sighișoara, Romania.

Thank you for reading my book.

If you enjoyed it, please take a moment to leave me a review at your favorite online retailer. Then, enjoy more adventures with Katie, Cam, and John in a preview of . . .

Faces in the Flames: A Ghost Story
(Book 1 of my Ghost Stories Series)

CHAPTER ONE

November 1944 – the Attack

"What the ...?" Cameron Lund said as he fell. Before he could finish, he landed on the gray steel deck of the ship. It happened so fast he didn't have time stop his fall. He had been sleeping in his bunk. His fall had woken him up. *Who was the wise guy,* he wondered? Looking around, he saw other shipmates on the deck too.

Lund scrambled to his feet. "What gives?" he yelled to nearby sailors.

"I think the ship's been hit," was the first reply. "Maybe an accident up forward," one guy said.

"Maybe . . .," but that thought was cut off. A second huge blast went off. The whole ship lifted up and then dropped down. At the same time, it rocked left and right. The power to move the 23,000 ton ship like that scared Lund. He grabbed the edge of his bunk to steady himself. Through an open hatch Lund could see the sky filled with flames. He looked at the hatch that led to the fire room. The fire room was where he worked aboard the ship. The boilers that powered the ship were there.

Lund turned to his friend, Bowers, who was just getting up. "Bowers . . . gotta get to our battle stations. This is big!"

Bowers started forward to the engine room hatch.

Lund only saw the back of his friend as Lund jumped through the fire room doorway. That was the last time he ever saw Bowers. Outside, hot oil rained down on everyone there. The sounds of the blasts echoed off the steel walls of the fire room.

Sailors were already in the fire room when Lund got there. Reed and Duffy were at their work stations. Lund went straight to his work station. He controlled the water going to the boilers. Too much water would flood a boiler. Too little water and the boiler would overheat and break down.

The fire room chief, Smitty, got there just after Lund. Smitty started directing the men. As they worked, more blasts outside increased their worries. Smitty sent Duffy topside to see what was going on with the ship. Almost right away, the blasts increased. The men were there for about 15 minutes. Lund prayed all the more with each explosion he heard.

As Lund worked near the hatch, the ship's captain stopped just outside. The captain yelled in to Lund, "Get off the ship. It's going down."

Lund didn't have to be told twice. It had been the longest 15-minutes of his life, so far. He yelled over to the men at the boilers, "The Captain said to let it go. She's going down!" So, the men quickly shut down all the boilers, except one. That one would supply some power to the ship if needed.

"Quick, out the starboard hatch!" Smitty ordered. But, when they opened the hatch on the right side of the ship, thick black smoke poured in. The men could barely breathe. They slammed the hatch shut. Then, the men ran over to the port side hatch. This left side hatch looked better. Only a small amount of smoke hovered in the hallway.

With the crazy things going on, the Chief forgot Duffy. The three men started towards the back of the ship. Suddenly, he remembered. "Wait, where's Duffy?" Smitty asked the men. Smitty wasn't sure if Duffy ever came back to the fire room. "Lund, go back and make sure Duffy got out of the fire room." Smitty and Reed started aft.

Lund stuck his head in the fire room hatch and yelled for Duffy. Lund didn't know Duffy was told to go topside. Lund could only see thick black smoke in the fire room from the hatchway. Lund knew it was no use. Duffy couldn't still be alive if he was down in the fire room.

That thick smoke now made it hard to see in the hallway. From somewhere, Lund heard a guy yell, "You can't go back aft. Fire is setting off the ammo there!"

Lund turned and said to himself, "Dear God, my mom's going to get word I'm dead." Just as he said this, a man ran through the smoke at the end of the hallway. Lund just barely saw him. *If that guy can make it out that way, maybe I can too.* So, Lund ran through the smoke, following the other man. He found his way to the lowest deck on the ship. He could see flames around the entire ship. Some of those flames were at least 200 feet high. There was just one slim wedge of water free of flames. He lowered himself over the side and swam out. Just beyond the edge of the flames were boats from nearby ships. One of the boats pulled Lund aboard.

From the small rescue boat, Lund could see men still on the sinking ship. Some men jumped into the burning water. He could see some trying to swim under the flames. He said a prayer for them as he helped pull men into the small boat. Still, some died there in the boat. He thought of the men dying inside the ship . . . alone. Their families would never know how they died.

Later that day, all the survivors got to a nearby ship. Lund found Reed. They looked for Chief Smitty and Duffy, but no one had seen them. They and his friend Bowers were never found. It was the saddest day of young Cameron Lund's life. On the ship, officers told the men more of what happened. It was then that Lund heard 63 men had died. It was an enemy suicide sub that hit them.

CHAPTER TWO

Adventure and Danger Comes Again Many Years Later

Why'd they have to sink that ship way out here? Cam asked in his head. *If the Germans had sunk it, we'd be there by now.* Cam looked down and shook his head left and right. He knew he was just being silly. He was just so tired of traveling. His drooping head and slumped shoulders showed it.

"Sorry, son. We've still got at least a couple more hours. Then we have to change to the next plane," Cam's dad said. He was just as tired of traveling as Cam. The seats in the plane lost their comfort a long time ago. He shifted in his seat. He had lost track himself as to how much longer they still had to go.

He looked over at his 15-year-old son, Cam. Bill Lund was proud of his son, Cam. He named Cam after his dad. He knew the trip was tough on Cam. He also knew it would be the trip of a lifetime.

Cam had loved his grandpa. He was Cam's hero. The old sailor had lots of stories. Cam would sit and listen to his grandpa talk about the past. His war stories sounded scary. He promised his grandpa that someday he would dive on his ship. He would see what his grandpa went through in the war.

Cam was average size for his age. His hair was a very light brown and he had blue eyes. He looked a lot like his grandpa did when he was that age.

"Things will be great when we get there," he told Cam. At least, that's what he hoped. Cam's dad always tried to look on the bright side of things. Arranging the trip had been a lot of work for Cam's dad. He had to get the okay from the chief at Ulithi. He had to explain why they wanted to dive on the shipwreck. The chief said yes, but the father and son would need to dive with local guides. The guides would meet the two when they got to Ulithi.

Ulithi is an atoll. An atoll is a group of tiny islands. A volcano makes the islands. The volcano forms a peak. The mountain peak grows up and out of the ocean. The peak is open in the middle, kind of like a donut. The peak forms a circle of small islands in the water. All this makes up an atoll. Ulithi Atoll is in the Pacific Ocean.

Cam had heard the travel plans, but now they seem so different. At first, it all sounded thrilling. He could barely believe it. His dad signed them up for SCUBA* diving lessons. His dad wanted them to SCUBA dive on a sunken ship. "Diving down so deep is risky. Of course, all SCUBA diving can be risky. That's why we must take lessons. We need to learn how to dive safely," Cam's dad had said to Cam. "But, diving is the only way to see the ship."

The sunken ship was the one Cam's grandpa served on. He was in the Navy during WWII*. Now, the ship sits in 130 feet of water. In WWII, a submarine sank the ship. In this case, they changed a torpedo into a sub. A man could steer the sub. The idea was to lose one man in order to sink a ship.

Cam had heard many stories from his grandpa about the ship. So, Cam knew there would be adventure. There had to be! Plus, maybe a little bit of danger. He figured he was ready for some danger, too.

He never thought he'd get bored on the trip. But now boredom washed over him in waves. The length of the trip seemed to grow with each passing second. He had doubts he would ever get to the adventure part. He was sure there couldn't be any danger left at this point. *Well, maybe the danger of dying from boredom*, he thought.

The trip was long. They had flown six hours to get to Los Angeles from Maryland. After that, they flew for 15 more hours. They took 3 planes before they, at last, got to the island of Yap. Each plane seemed to be smaller and smaller than the one before. The thrill of the trip faded as time stretched on. It felt like they were traveling to the end of the earth.

When Cam and his dad got to Yap Island, things changed for them. They felt like they were entering a different world. All the plants and trees were extra green and there were lots of them. The view looked like a scene from out of one of Cam's video games. As they got off the plane, the thick, damp air was like a wall of water. *That's why things grow so well here*, thought Cam. *The air is so damp. You never feel that in a video game. I guess no one would buy one if they did.* He gave a short chuckle to his own joke.

His wet clothes and skin took his mind off his joke right away. Cam felt awful. He went into the airport building as fast as he could. He hoped the air would be dryer inside.

Cam was out of luck. The small building had no air-conditioning. The air inside was just a little dryer. Cam sat down and watched their bags.

Many people sat in the small terminal. Cam noticed a pretty, young girl in the crowd. She had rich dark skin and long brown hair. He hoped to meet some kids his age. *Of course, meeting pretty girls like her would be even better*, he thought.

Cam looked around for his dad. He saw him not far away near a big sign. The sign read *Pacific Missionary Airlines*. Under the sign was a simple looking desk. Behind the desk stood a man in a short-sleeved white shirt, and black slacks. Next to him was a woman in a while top and black shorts. She had an airline badge on her top. Cam's dad talked to the man and then shook his hand. Then, the man pointed to a small doorway.

Cam's dad walked back to Cam with a smile on his face. He said, "Come on. We can go get on the plane now." Cam was a bit surprised. They didn't have to wait for an announcement to board the plane. Cam picked up his bags, relieved this would be the last leg of the trip. His dad picked up the other bags and led the way to the door.

Cam wondered, *shouldn't we have checked these bags in? Doesn't the airline have to load them on the plane?* He thought it odd, but his dad didn't say anything. Cam followed dragging his bags.

They walked back out into the hot, damp air. Cam saw the man who had been at the desk. He was taking the bags from Cam's dad. He carried them twenty feet and then set them down. Cam looked around. He expected to see a jet plane, but none were there. Parked in front of them was a very small, 8-passenger plane. The plane was nice and clean but was very small. It really didn't look like it could hold a lot of dive gear. The plane barely looked able to hold the three of them. Cam had never been on such a small plane before.

"Are we going to fit on that plane?" Cam asked his dad. "Is there room for us?" He worried there might be some big guy in the seat next to him. It had happened on an earlier flight.

"I'm not so sure, Cam," his dad said. Then, he gave a slight chuckle and shake of his head. "But, I promise you, this is the last plane we need to take to get there." Cam's dad was tired of the traveling too. He welcomed the last leg of the trip. "But, remember, this is where the adventure begins."